SPECIAL MESSAGE TO READERS

This book is published under the auspices of
THE ULVERSCROFT FOUNDATION
(registered charity No. 264873 UK)

Established in 1972 to provide funds for
research, diagnosis and treatment of eye diseases.
Examples of contributions made are: —

A Children's Assessment Unit at
Moorfield's Hospital, London.

•

Twin operating theatres at the
Western Ophthalmic Hospital, London.

•

A Chair of Ophthalmology at the
Royal Australian College of Ophthalmologists.

•

The Ulverscroft Children's Eye Unit at the
Great Ormond Street Hospital For Sick Children,
London.

You can help further the work of the Foundation
by making a donation or leaving a legacy. Every
contribution, no matter how small, is received
with gratitude. Please write for details to:

**THE ULVERSCROFT FOUNDATION,
The Green, Bradgate Road, Anstey,
Leicester LE7 7FU, England.
Telephone: (0116) 236 4325
In Australia write to:
THE ULVERSCROFT FOUNDATION,
c/o The Royal Australian College of
Ophthalmologists,
27, Commonwealth Street, Sydney,
N.S.W. 2010.**

SIDEWINDER

All Flynn wants is to be Marshall of Tucson, but he is framed by the territory's richest rancher, Frank Buchanan, and thrown into Yuma prison. Five years later Flynn comes out, intent on clearing his name and burning for vengeance. Fists thud, knives flash and bullets fly as he rides both sides of the law and participates in kidnapping and double-dealing. He is once again arrested for a murder of which he is innocent. Can he escape the noose a second time?

JOHN DYSON

SIDEWINDER

0026700832

Complete and Unabridged

LINFORD
Leicester

First published in Great Britain in 1998 by
Robert Hale Limited
London

First Linford Edition
published 1999
by arrangement with
Robert Hale Limited
London

British Library CIP Data

Dyson, John, *1943* –
  Sidewinder.—Large print ed.—
  Linford western library
  1. Western stories
  2. Large type books
  I. Title
  823.9'14 [F]

ISBN 0–7089–5492–8

Published by
F. A. Thorpe (Publishing) Ltd.
Anstey, Leicestershire

Set by Words & Graphics Ltd.
Anstey, Leicestershire
Printed and bound in Great Britain by
T. J. International Ltd., Padstow, Cornwall

This book is printed on acid-free paper

1

The bullet whined and whistled past my head, chipping rocks, the crack of the explosion bouncing back and forth off the walls of the canyon. Close. Too close for comfort. The sun glinted on the rifle of the look-out up in the rocks. Slowly I raised my right hand and held my bronc steady with my knees, the reins held high in my left. The bell of the Casa Grande ranch house began clanging. They were well fortified against attack. The man on the rock signalled back up the canyon. Soon I heard the rattle of iron-shod hooves on stone and five riders swirled into a halt around me.

'What do you want?' one snarled.

'I got business with Mr Buchanan.'

'Yeah? Come on.'

The ranch was a collection of adobe shacks clustered around the centrepiece of an imposing two-storey house built Spanish-style. It had a wide veranda beneath shady colonnades at the front, set back behind adobe walls with gunports behind which a couple of guards skulked. They opened the iron gates and let me through.

This place was built like a fort. It could withstand Apache attack, or even the US Cavalry, come to that. It was the home or hide-out, of the richest man in Arizona Territory. Some said he was worth a million dollars, which was a lot of gelt in that part of the country.

'I'll see if the boss will see you,' one of the riders muttered, and went inside.

'He'd better,' I said, as I sat my horse. 'I've come a long way.'

A girl was sitting on the top bar of the corral. She was no more than about thirteen, dressed in jeans, blouse and bandanna like a cowboy, with a revolver stuck in her belt and a Spencer carbine in her hand.

'You a lawman?' she called. 'What you want with my daddy?'

'That's between me and him.'

She had corn-coloured hair and her eyes were a mixture of feline greens and greys. She had full cheeks, a pert nose, and petulant lips, the lower one stuck out in a rebellious way. I couldn't help thinking she was a sexy little thing, even if she was half my age and just a kid. I had also heard she was a spoilt bitch, who ordered the men around like skivvies and had her own way.

'What's your name?' she asked, as she swung the carbine on me and thumbed the hammer.

'Sean,' I said. 'Sean Flynn. What's yours?'

'Lily.' She spoke proudly. 'Lily Buchanan.'

'Nice name, Lily. Pure and virginal. I hope you live up to it.'

She showed her middle teeth in a scoffing grin. 'Get lost, creep.'

'He'll see you,' the man called from the house doorway and stepped down.

Buchanan was the biggest freight haulage operator in the Territory, with an army of wagons and teamsters. This beef ranch was just a sideline. He had a finger in a lot of pies, including a new stage run from Tombstone. He was the leader of the notorious Tucson Ring, the shadowy group of businessmen who decided *who* ran *what* in Arizona. Nobody worked without their say-so. Buchanan had the government contract to ship in supplies to the army and the Indian reservations. That's what I had been investigating.

The ranch house was cool and spacious, Navaho rugs on the floors, heavily ornate tables and chairs, racks of rifles along the walls. Buchanan was sitting in a polished leather armchair, one boot crooked over his knee. He was a big man, with a heavy moustache, his face the same colour as the leather and as hard-looking.

'What can I do for you, Marshal?' he said.

I strode towards him, my right hand

outstretched. He put his own up with an air of surprise as if to shake mine. As he did so I crammed a warrant into his horny palm, slapped it tight with my left hand.

'This is a warrant for you to appear at Tucson courthouse to answer nine charges of corruption and fraud. It's served.'

'What?' He threw it on to his desk like it was red hot. 'What the hell you talkin' about?'

There was a pale, frail-looking woman in a shawl sitting by the fireplace. 'What is it, Frank?'

I tipped my hat to her. 'You are a witness that this has been served, ma'am.'

'You leave my wife out of this.'

'What does he want?' she said, weakly. 'What have you done, Frank?'

'Go to your room, Amy, I can handle this.' He spoke kindly at first, but snapped, impatiently. 'Go on.'

As she rose, his wife was racked with coughing, and I saw the splash of blood

5

on her handkerchief. Consumption. A Mexican woman in black helped her out.

'What's all this about?' Buchanan growled, when we were alone.

'You know what it's about. It's about the numerous consignments of beef, flour and tools earmarked for the Camp Verde Reservation that never arrived. It's about the way you and the Indian agent, Ferguson, have been stealing the Apaches' entitlement and selling it to line your own pockets. It's about corruption that goes all the way up the line to Washington. It's about the way you bribed the quartermaster of the Tucson garrison; how supplies destined for the 10th Cavalry somehow disappeared.'

Buchanan laughed, cool and arrogant, struck a match on his boot, and lit a cigar. 'Go to hell.'

'The warrant's served. You'd better be there. Ferguson only got his job because he's the no-good nephew of a senator. The weak-gutted rat has spilled the beans on you, Buchanan. I've got all the evidence I need.'

'What are you, an Injin-lover? Who cares if a few lousy Apaches didn't get their meal? Who cares if they all starve to death? You think a jury's gonna care? Come on, boy, use some sense. You and I can come to an agreement over this.' He opened a drawer, took out a wallet and began to flick through a wad of greenbacks. 'How much? A thousand enough?'

I had to smile at the man's sheer gall. 'You may be able to bribe the Arizona senator, maybe even the governor for all I know, but you can't have everybody in your pocket. It ain't so much the Apaches I'm bothered about, although it's men like you who have stirred up all the trouble in the Territory. I just happen in a small way to represent the taxpayers of the United States. It's them you've been cheating. I'm doing my job, Buchanan, so you can put your wallet away.'

'You jumped-up bog-trotter,' he

roared, springing to his feet, jabbing a forefinger at my chest. 'You dare to come in here, come into my home? I'll rip you apart. You haven't got a chance. You think that tin badge gives you protection? You'll find out.'

I braced myself and stood my ground, although the prodding finger was getting on my nerves and the look on his face was sheer malice. 'I'll forget attempted bribery and threatening a law officer. I got enough to go on.'

'You — ' He spluttered out obscenities. 'You're as good as dead.'

I turned on my heel, pulled on my gloves and, spurs jangling on the stone floor, ambled out of there, out into the blast of sunshine. I climbed on to my bronc, mustering as much coolness as I could, and prepared to ride out. Buchanan had followed me and Lily ran over to him.

'What's the matter, Pa?' He pulled her into his broad arm, and she simpered up at him, 'You want me to kill him?

'Let the little rat go,' Buchanan snarled. 'He'll get what's coming to him.'

As I rode towards the gate, through men with menace in their eyes, a carbine barked, a slug spurted the dust, making my horse whinny and whirl. I turned and saw Lily with the carbine aimed at me. Her father slowly pushed the barrel aside. For moments we stared at each other. 'Open the gates,' he shouted.

Whoo! I sure was pleased that assignment was over. I put spurs to the bronc and headed back towards Tucson.

2

I guess Buchanan could have killed me, or had me killed. Plenty of lawmen had gotten bloodily blasted in the course of their duty. But, even in this wild, untamed territory killing a US marshal was not an enterprise any man took lightly. If there was one thing on which all lawmen were agreed, it was to track down the killer of a colleague. Buchanan liked hob-nobbing with the bigwigs at the governor's ball too much to chance putting his head in a noose. At least, that's how I figured.

It was going to be hard making my case stick. I was going to need enough solid evidence that even if he tried to buy every juryman they would be unable to turn a blind eye. So I decided to investigate the spate of robberies of the Buchanan Stage Line. It was odd that the road agents seemed to know every time a large consignment of silver bullion was being transported from the Tombstone mines towards Tucson. And odder that they always got clean away. It was time to ride 'shotgun' on the stage, but I would be carrying a 12-shot Winchester repeater carbine, and a brace of Colt .45s.

I explained my plan to the marshal at Tombstone, a man called Earp. He was a tall, clear-eyed dude who liked to dress city-style in a four-button suit and curly-brimmed derby. He and his brothers had reputations as gamblers and fast guns, and they had their hands full with the Clanton clan. Earp wished me luck and told the stage line that on this occasion there would be no passengers and I would be riding shotgun.

The hills and valleys around Tombstone were crawling with no-goods and desperadoes intent on parting the hard-working miners from their cash. Word had got out that we were carrying a strong-box, some $10,000 worth of silver. I had a strong feeling that the word came from Buchanan, himself, that he was robbing his own stage line. I needed to capture one of the agents red-handed and make him talk. Trouble was not long in coming.

The driver, George Hutchins, a noncommittal, ornery bustard, in a Stetson and duster coat, was hanging onto the reins of the four-horse team who were kicking up dust, going at a good lick, when I heard the reports of revolvers and, looking back, saw six riders galloping down out of the hills towards the dust trail, closing in on us on either side.

'Give 'em the lash, George,' I shouted. 'We'll make a run for it.'

I crouched down and aimed my Winchester, determined that I was going to be one 'shotgun' who didn't hit the dust. The small open coach was swaying and bouncing, the bullets from the horsemen buzzing about us, but not doing much damage. I squeezed the trigger and saw one of the riders catapulted from his horse.

Damn! I thought. He's dead! What I wanted to do was wing one. I needed a road agent who would talk, tell us who had hired them, who the silver would go to. We were rattling along and it wasn't easy to get a good bead. Puffs of powdersmoke filled the air as I pumped the lever and fired some more. The robbers were gaining on us, but I was pretty certain I could out-shoot them.

'Whoa!' George hollered and began to haul on the reins.

'What's the matter?' I shouted, glancing at him as the stagecoach began to slow. The trail ahead was flat and empty. 'Keep these critters going. Give 'em the whip.'

I was about to return to my shooting when, from the corner of my eye, I saw George's elbow raised, a revolver in his fist. He back-handed me across the temple, and hit me again. Suddenly, the world faded away . . .

13

When I came to I was slumped in the seat inside the stage. What had happened? I was pinioned by my wrists to the window rail, trussed with my own handcuffs. And another pair of irons locked my ankles around my boots. The stage was going back through the hills towards Tombstone. I shouted up at George but there was no reply. What'n hell was he playing at?

When we rolled back into Tombstone's dusty main street, and I heard Hutchins hollering that we had been robbed, folks came running to see what was going on. The driver jumped down and pointed a finger at me.

'He was in cahoots with 'em. He made me stop the coach, hand over the bullion. When they had gone he was about to kill me, but I got in first, buffaloed him.'

It's amazing what folks will believe. They hardly gave me a chance to tell my side of things. They looked like they were ready to lynch me then and there. I was glad to see Wyatt Earp come from the saloon and shoulder his way through the crowd. George Hutchins was a big, blustering man who had been driving the stage for a couple of years and was well known in the town, whereas I came from Tucson and was a foreigner to most of them. It was not unknown for a lawman to ride both sides and they looked like they were glad to have proof of it.

'I'm gonna have to take you in, Flynn,' Earp said, unlocking me. 'I'll put you up before the magistrate in the morning. You can tell your side of the story.'

'You don't mean you're taking his word against mine?' I protested. 'He's been put up to it. Buchanan's behind all this.'

The crowd laughed at the absurdity of such an idea and followed along to watch me being thrown into the lockup. I had put a few men behind bars myself in five years as a deputy and marshal. This was not an experience I enjoyed. I spent a miserable night wondering what my chances were. Earp ignored me and returned to his poker game. Could it be that even he was in the employ of Buchanan's gang? Why didn't he get up a posse, go after the road agents, try to get the bullion back? They hadn't got much of a start.

In the morning I was marched into court. Hutchins was there, sullen and dour in his demeanour. He repeated his allegations. I told the judge that it was Hutchins who was the crook. I scowled over at him. I was ready to jump over there and knock his teeth down his throat.

The judge mopped his face with a bandanna and gave me a severe look. 'Young man, in view of the fact that you are a lawman and due to the conflicting evidence, this case will be dismissed. I should warn you that if anything should befall George Hutchins you will be the prime suspect. Is that understood?'

'Sure, it's understood,' I said. 'It means that he's getting away scot free. Is this your idea of justice? How do you think I am going to do my job?'

'Come on,' Earp said, taking my arm. As we emerged into the street I saw Hutchins mounting a horse and going at a fast lope out of town. 'Leave him be, Flynn. You heard the judge.'

'You make me sick,' I said, pulling my arm away. 'I'm going back to Tucson.'

'Take it easy,' he warned. 'Buchanan's a dangerous man to come up against.'

* * *

Just how dangerous I found out two weeks later. George Hutchins was discovered with his throat slit and a knife in his back in a Tucson alley. My knife. It had a curious carved handle and had once belonged to an Apache. I had been wondering where it had gotten to. Now I knew.

My own deputy, Ned Parsons, arrested

17

me at the adobe shack I rented on the outskirts of town. He was a likeable tousle-headed kid, but he had a serious look and a jut to his jaw.

'I gotta do this, Sean,' he apologized, putting the cuffs on me. 'We got a tip off to search this place.'

He and another deputy searched my few belongings but found nothing except ten silver dollars, the remains of my month's pay. They took me round the back and Ned took a look down a disused well. He climbed out hauling a sack and whistled when he peeked inside. It was the biggest part of the stolen bullion, clearly stamped with the mine's name. I was back in the poky again.

* * *

They didn't waste a lot of time at my trial, in spite of my protestations that I had been framed. The jury looked unimpressed when I told them that Frank Buchanan was behind it

18

all, behind the stage robberies, the swindling of the Apaches out of their due rations, the pilfering of army property.

A ripple of amusement ran through the onlookers when I pointed at Buchanan in the public gallery and shouted out, 'That man's greed is the cause of most of the bloodshed in this territory. He *wants* the army to be brought in. It's good for business.'

Ned Parsons was the only man to stand up for me. He said that I had an unblemished five-year record as a lawman, that he respected the way I had carried out my duties, and that he did not think I would be fool enough to leave my own knife in Hutchins, or stash the silver in my own backyard when there was the whole of Arizona to hide it in.

The prosecuting lawyer smiled in his snide fashion. 'Well, you would say that, wouldn't you?' he said. 'You stick together.'

All I remember was the jury filing in

to say they found me guilty of armed robbery, but brought in an open verdict on the slaying. All I remember was that dim, dusty room, the staring eyes, the sneer on Buchanan's face, the judge banging his gavel, his words ringing into my brain: ' . . . five years hard labour.'

★ ★ ★

Chained hand and foot I was loaded into the cagewagon that would transport me through blistering heat more than 300 miles to Yuma prison. I was almost glad that my poor mother was long-dead and did not have to witness my humiliation.

It was probably the most sickening sensation of my life when the prison gates slammed behind me and I found myself in another world, a world of brutal guards and depraved, dehumanized prisoners. My head shaved, I was clothed in the rough, striped uniform and marched to the communal adobe cell that was to be my home for the next five years. As the door was locked behind me I looked into the sneering eyes of my fellow prisoners as they lay on their double bunks, crammed in that stinking hole like cattle in wagons.

'Well, look who's here,' one growled, getting to his feet, his fists clenched. 'The Tucson marshal.' I recognized him as a sadist I had put in this place for the murder of a Mexican, the rape of his young daughter.

It's not going to be easy here, I thought, before they started pummelling and kicking me.

3

The days were bad enough. The guards with their guns and billy-sticks cursed and hit us for no reason. The chains chafed our ankles; the ugly, rough clothes and shorn hair. Every day we went shambling out to the quarry to crush rocks with sledgehammers in a heat that soared to 120°F as the sun climbed high. All we thought about was the next break to be ladled out a few drops of water, to make it through the day. I even looked forward to the bowl of greasy slop they called food. The days were not the problem. If a man was tough enough he could get through them without keeling over. It was the nights I dreaded.

To be herded into one of those stinking, stultifying adobe cell blocks, to be locked in for the night with nothing to do or think about was bad enough, to have time on their hands brought out the most sadistic and base instincts in men, especially men like these who were crude, ignorant and malicious to begin with. Most of them blamed the system for their being there. And I was a representative of that system, a lawman. Their new game was to torment me. There were a few men who took no part, but the majority were too gutless to oppose the ringleaders. If they did not participate they laughed as my punishment began. All I wanted was to lie on my hard bunk and ease away the ache in my bones from the long day. But they wanted to play.

My main torturer was the thick-necked sadist who had first greeted me. Built like a gorilla, he had little hair on his skull, but he made up for it with the fur sprouting all over his body. He would have been a good candidate for that missing link the professors argue about. His forehead receded backwards, a good indication of his minimal brain. His red-rimmed piggy-eyes burned with hatred for me. He didn't speak, he grunted, and every word was preceded by some foul epithet. He had the humour of a child who liked to pull legs off spiders. His name was Bolton, Dave Bolton. He thought himself very funny as he began taunting me. I tried to ignore the insults, the barrage of sneering remarks that went on and on. If I replied I knew the beating would begin. Eventually he got to me, as he would every night. I lost my rag and I had to fight. Bolton and his bully boys cornered me and I fought with everything I had. I learned to go for the eyes, the testicles, I punched; I chopped with the flat of my hand, I elbowed into guts; I kicked out at grinning black teeth, but there were too many for me. When they had me helpless, face down, they tried to think of new ways to hurt me, and humiliate me.

In this prison, unsupervised once they were locked in, men without women looked elsewhere for sex. If you were young and pretty you didn't have much chance. You were claimed as the punk of one of these thugs. I wasn't exactly pretty, but I was young, twenty-four years old when I went inside, and my body lean and well-formed. My main fear was of being raped. That's why I fought . . . so frantically.

The Mexican, Jaime Ostos, had had a patch of dusty land a couple of miles outside Tucson. His wife had died in childbirth and he somehow managed to scratch a living with his mule, his well, his patch of maize and melons. I sometimes called in to see how he was getting along and he always welcomed me with old-fashioned Spanish hospitality, offering food and drink in spite of his poverty. He had a young daughter who, the last time I saw him alive, was about twelve. Mercedes was her name. She was wild, skinny, with a mop of tousled black hair and cheeky smile. They had managed to survive in that harsh land, even survive Apache attacks. Until the day Bolton rode in.

Even when I arrested him for smashing in Jaime's skull, for brutally raping and half strangling Mercedes, he seemed to think he had a grievance. 'They were only Greasers,' he said. 'What's the matter with you?' He couldn't understand why I clubbed him with the butt of my carbine before I locked him up. Maybe I shouldn't have done that but I was sickened by the senseless slaughter. He was a petty crook who preyed on the weak and defenceless and bragged about it. He didn't have the brains to cover his tracks.

Anyhow, Bolton had drawn ten years for homicide and rape and I well remembered him raging at me from the dock that he would be back, that he would kill me. One of my deputies drove him in the cage along to Yuma. I found a place for Mercedes living-in with a Tucson widow lady. And went on with my investigations into Frank Buchanan. I never imagined that Dave Bolton and I would come face to face so soon afterwards.

When they had kicked my ribs and twisted my arms and had their fun, I was left to crawl back into my bunk. I would lay in a semi-conscious trance and wish I could just float out of there, float away through the bars, away up into the darkness. But from where I was I couldn't even see the stars. I missed seeing the stars. All I could see were the grunting, farting, snoring, cursing, muttering shapes of my fellow prisoners. When I had been brought in here I had youthful optimistic ideas. I had believed in decency, in helping to forge a civilized society in this wilderness. Gradually I was becoming as hard and ugly as these creatures.

Anybody who has not been locked up with a bunch of criminally-insane sadists can have little idea of the constant pressure, the fear. You either go under or, as in the animal world, you fight for pecking position. I became convinced that my only way out was to get rid of Bolton.

A fortunate find in the rock yard was a rusty metal spike. My heart began thudding when I picked it up without being noticed. Whenever I got a few seconds alone I honed it on a rock to a sharp point. I harboured it in a secret crevice in the yard. It was more important to me than a bag of diamonds. I waited my chance. When it came I took it. I heard one of the warders at supper one night, tell Bolton to carry out a bin of offal that had gone rancid in the heat, was too bad even for us, to throw it on the rubbish heap. I slipped out on the pretence of going to the john. I caught him in the alley behind the canteen building. He had the empty bin in one hand.

'Hi,' I whispered. 'I've been looking for you. It's just you and me now.'

He grunted with puzzlement when he saw the spike in my fist. He hurled the bin at me. I dodged aside, parried the blow he threw, and stuck him like a pig. He squealed. I savoured his fear, his pain, his panic.

'How's it feel?' I asked as I plunged the iron spike in again and again. He took a long time dying.

When I was done I tossed the spike away, wiped the blood from my hands on his clothing and went back to the canteen. The men were being lined up ready to be put into their cells. I felt like a great weight had been taken from my shoulders. I felt like I was floating, light and free.

Of course, I was the chief suspect. The guards worked me over but I wouldn't confess. They tossed me into solitary, a narrow black hole with no room to stand. At first I was glad of the change. Even the rats in that dark dungeon were preferable to the human rats whose cell I shared. A lot of men broke in the black hole, went crazy, not knowing whether it was night or day, how long they had been there, how long they would have to stay. I did hundreds of push-ups in an attempt to keep my body sound. I spoke out loud all the law statutes I had memorized in my job as marshal. Somehow I stayed sane. At least, I think I did. Perhaps I did turn a little bit crazy after six weeks in there.

I couldn't stand without being held up, I couldn't bear the harsh sunlight in my eyes, blinding me, when they dragged me out. They dragged me before the prison governor, but I still refused to crack. I simply recited my rights as a prisoner, demanded that an appeal be opened into my case, that I be allowed to write to my lawyer kid-brother. I denied any knowledge of how Bolton got stabbed. All I said was, 'Whoever did it did the world a service.'

After that they didn't bother me any more. Those desperadoes looked at me with a new light in their eyes. A look of respect. Some even tried to befriend me. I didn't want the friendship of those scum. I was still a loner in the barracks cell, but I was also top dog, or top hyena, or whatever I had become.

4

It seemed unbelievable but five years passed. Every long day, every even longer night passed. I counted each one, marked off each passing year, wondered what was happening beyond those high walls. To be thrown into the hell-hole of Yuma prison was not an experience any man would relish. To be thrown out after five years of living in close confinement with foul-mouthed perverts and killers was not easy, either. Don't get me wrong, I was more than glad to get out of there, to have survived. But the prospect of being so suddenly free and on my own kinda gave me the collywobbles. What should I do?

'How about my gunbelt, my rifle?' I asked the governor.

'Confiscated by the government,' he grunted. 'You don't think we're gonna give you back the tools to go out and commit more robberies, more murders?'

'I didn't commit any robberies or murders,' I gritted out at him as I pocketed my few valuables, my watch, my ten silver dollars I had when I was arrested.

'Yeah,' the fat pig yawned. 'So you been telling me every year. But the jury found otherwise.'

Everything was in order, I had to admit that. They gave me back my clothes, my wool shirt, bandanna, Levi jeans, my fringed shotgun chaps, my spurs, my boots, my buckskin jacket and my old Stetson hat. It was good to get back into them after living in stinking striped prison garb.

'What about my bronc?'

'How the hell should I know what happened to your bronc? You were transported here in the paddy wagon. Maybe your bronc's still waitin' for you in Tucson.'

The guards laughed harshly at that.

'How the hell am I supposed to get back to Tucson in this heat without a horse, without guns?'

It was practically a death sentence. Three hundred and thirty-five miles of mesquite, sagebrush and desert on foot would be bad enough. That was without taking into account the possibility of renegade Apaches or the frontier scum who infested the foothills. Plenty of them might well have a grudge against a former lawman.

'Don't play your violin to us, Flynn,' the governor snapped out. 'You shoulda thought of that before you got sent here in the first place.'

'I was set up, you know that.'

'Yeah, yeah. If I were you I'd forget that old tune. If you're thinking of vengeance, forget that, too. You're all washed up in this territory. Take my advice, get across the Colorado river, start a new life in California.'

Vengeance? What else had I been thinking of for five years, every day, every night, but vengeance on those bastards who had sent me here, the judge, the jury, with their smug, comfortable lives? And Frank Buchanan. Particularly Buchanan. It wasn't just justice I wanted any more. I wanted to see him suffer.

'You won't see me back,' I said. 'But I wouldn't like to be in the shoes of them who railroaded me.'

'Aw, Jeez,' the governor groaned. 'Throw him out.'

When the big studded door creaked closed, and I was alone on the outside, I tell you, it was an awesome experience. The big blue sky above. The desert stretching out in front of me. Free. At last. It was real scary.

★ ★ ★

Maybe the governor was right. If I had had any sense I would have turned west, walked to the little port on the banks of the river, took the ferry over to the other side. Or maybe worked my way round to California on a

34

sail-steamer that brought supplies into Arizona Territory. But I was never one for taking advice. Nor did I ever have much sense. I started walking . . . east . . . into the desert. Back into my past.

Maybe five years in poky had sent me crazy? I didn't even have any water for Chrissake! The noon sun was burning down, and at a temperature of over 100° on the Fahrenheit scale, my sweat was already dampening my shirt. No man could live without water or a horse out in the desert for long. Maybe I hoped the stage from Los Angeles to Tucson would come along and my few dollars would purchase me a seat on top. But I knew it only passed once in every ten days and maybe it had passed yesterday?

I kept on walking, out along the trail towards those blue-folded mountains. My high-heel boots weren't made for walking and after three hours I'd had enough. My clothes were sticking to me and my mouth as dry as dust. Even in the prison quarry, as we sledged the rocks, they gave us water on the hour. So I took a rest. Maybe it would be better to travel by night, especially if there were any hostiles about.

Time passed. It was too hot to sit down, so I squatted on my heels in the shade of a big rock and pitched stones at the lizards who crept up to look at me, flickering their tongues. I guess they and I had nothing better to do.

Suddenly I heard an awful cater-wauling. Someone coming along the trail in a cloud of dust. I froze, my first thoughts that it might be a band of drunken Indians. But it was a drunken white man. I watched as the mule train appeared out of the quavering mirage of heat.

It was a wonderful sight, twenty mules in pairs straining at their harness collars pulling two high-sided wagons at a steady pace, their bells ringing out. A greybearded 'skinner' was swaying back and forth on the wagon tongue, a battered hat lop-sided on his head, a bottle of whiskey in his paw. He was yelling some saloon song about 'Sweet Rosie of Allybammy'.

'Hold on,' he shouted when he saw me, pulling in on the jerk line. These were smart, well-trained mules and he came to a halt alongside me. 'Sean Flynn? Is that you, Marshal? What the divil you doin' here?'

'Ain't a marshal no more, Sam.' He was a local character I'd known vaguely five years before, in fact been forced to lock up once or twice for his own good. 'I done my time in Yuma. They thrown me out. I need a ride to Tucson.'

'Well, do ye now?' He wiped sweat from his nose tip with the back of his hand and scratched at his beard with the bottle neck. 'I ain't sure the company allows me to take aboard convicts.'

'Come on, Sam. You cain't leave me to walk.'

'I cain't, cain't I?' He reached out for a shotgun hooked into the corner of the wagon, waggled it, one-handed my way. 'You jest back off. I heard about what you done.'

'That was all lies.'

'Thass what they all say.'

'For Chrissake stop pointing that thing at me.'

'No reason why I shouldn't blow a hole through your insides, varmint like you. Keep back, young feller. Don't try none of your tricks.'

I grabbed the shotgun out of harm's way and he more or less toppled into my arms. 'You take it easy, Sam. You look like you could do with a rest.'

'Yeah,' he said, his knees caving, teetering as I held him up. 'I guess I could. Can you handle this rig?'

'I sure can try. Where's your swamper?'

'He ran off, said I weren't fit — ' Sam suddenly looked sorry for himself. 'Don't you go using the black snake on my babies. No need for that.'

'How do I git 'em to move,

otherwise?' I glanced up at the fifteen-foot whip coiled from the corner post.

'Plenty of cussin' does the trick.' He touched a sack of stones hung from the wagon tongue. 'If you got difficulty jest reach in here and toss a couple at that white mare, my lead lady, Esmeralda. That'll git her goin' and t'others'll follow.'

'You jest sleep it off, old-timer.' I put a hand under his rump and shoved him up into the back of the first wagon. He disappeared beneath the tarpaulin, muttering.

How we could manage down the steep gradients without a brake man on the second wagon I didn't know. But as far as I remembered the next twenty miles was pretty flat. Maybe we could make Collins Well by nightfall. After that we could worry. Luckily today there would be no bends or tricky canyons to manoeuvre through. All I had to do was follow a straight rutted line heading away across the desert.

Sam popped his toothless head out

from the tarpaulin, proffered the bottle. 'You wanna sup?'

'Nah,' I said. 'Not in this heat. I ain't had none in five years. I can wait. All I need is a mouthful of water from your barrel.'

'Help yourself, Marshal.' He bobbed down again.

I jumped up on to the tongue and yelled at the mules to hit the road. They just stood there flickering their ears. 'Shee-it! Ornery critters!' I took out a handful of stones and shied one hard up along at the white mule. It missed. So did the second. The third got her on the rump. 'Es-mer-al-da! Haugh!' And suddenly the whole team was taking the strain and the great heavy wagons were lumbering on their way. I reached for the whip and sent it snaking and cracking over their ears to encourage them. They broke into a trot. We were on our way.

Soon I began to get the hang of it. It felt good to be out in God's open air doing something useful at last.

A hundred and fifty feet of mules stretched out in front of me, going at their stiff-legged jog, with only the jerk line running from my hands through the hame rings of the nearside mules, clear to the bit ring of the near-leader. A steady pull on the line and a 'Haw!' turned the near-leader left, several jerks on the line and the shout of 'Gee!' turned them to the right. The jockey-stick fastened to the collar of the near-leader stretched across to the off-leader and made him follow the mare's turns. You had to cuss, of course. They expected it. They wouldn't go without it. It let them know you were still there. Yes, these sure were smart mules. I was almost tempted to try making them do a U-turn, see if they would skip over the line, like I'd watch them do when they came into town. But, I guessed that would be a mite ambitious.

Gradually we ate up the miles, the wheels of the heavy wagons creaking and grumbling until the sun set behind me and the desert was lit by a roseate afterglow. We hadn't made Collins Well but it was time to bed down before thick night set in. I managed to haul the mules in and looked under the canvas. Sam was snoring lustily and could not be woken. It looked like it was down to me. I found some sacks of split corn, and a pile of canvas mats. Maybe I shoulda unharnessed the mules, but I was worried they might all run off. I left them standing, arranged their mats out in front of them, and gave them each a good portion of corn, working backwards from Esmeralda. There was some jostling and biting, but generally they were as good as gold. By the time I got them all watered the stars were out.

There was some flour and coffee in a box hanging from the back of the second wagon so I made a fire of dried sagebrush sticks and put a flapjack in the ashes to bake. By the time I had a tin mug of coffee to my lips old Sam stuck his head out and groaned, 'Where am I?'

'Guess about thirty miles from Yuma.' I broke off some hot flapjack and passed it to him. 'You sure laid one on.'

'Guess I did.' His hands were shaking as he refilled the mug from the pot. 'Man needs a drink. Why them mules in harness?'

'I ain't no teamster. They've had their grub.'

He cussed and ambled over, bandy-legged, to unharness them. He hobbled the bunch-quitters with rawhide rope around the forelegs so they could only hop about in an ungainly way. Seemed hard on the poor critters but it allowed them to forage among the undergrowth without going far.

He had dug out another bottle by the time he got back. 'You sure that's wise?' I said.

'Sure.' He took a good pull and passed it to me. 'I'll be fine by marnin'.'

The whiskey was the real McCoy and tasted good. Clear and strong, it burned through me putting fire in my veins. It was like meeting an old friend again. The rock against my back was warm from the heat of the day, the night breeze was cool, and the fire merry. I listened to the eerie cries of night creatures out in the dark, kit foxes, coyotes, long-eared owls. It for certain was good to be free.

'So you figure you was framed?' Sam tossed me a blanket and settled down beside me. 'Huccome?'

'All I know is the hell of five wasted years in that place for somethun' I didn't do.' I spat into the flames, spat out the bitterness in me. 'Why, what's it to you?'

'I bet it weren't much fun in Yuma, you bein' a lawman an' all.'

'You can say that again.' I snatched the bottle from him and took another swallow that made my mind swirl and hatred swell up through me like bile. 'Somebody's gotta pay and I know who that somebody is.'

'Like who?'

'Who do you work for, Sam?'

'Arizona Haulage Company. Biggest operation in the territ'ry.'

'Who's your big boss?'

'Frank Buchanan owns the whole caboodle.'

'He's the one.'

'You gawn plumb loco? You wanna get them ideas outa your head, son, 'less you're lookin' fer a dose of lead poison.'

'Yeah, maybe. What's new, Sam?'

'His wife passed away. Been on her last legs a long time. Buchanan's gotten more mean and moody than ever since her death. Not that I ever see much of him. Jest what I hear. You want to stay clear of that varmint.'

'I'm not planning on breaking the law,' I muttered, as much to myself as to Sam. 'But I'm going to be even with that man. None so mighty as can't be toppled. Somehow I'll pin him. And if he wants violence I'm ready for him.'

'You wouldn't stand a snowball's chance in hell. He's got some hired killer riding for him. They reckon he's snake fast.'

'I can use a gun, myself. How about that daughter of his?'

'That li'l hellcat? Stay clear of her, too. Her daddy dotes on her. So she thinks she can ride roughshod over everybody.'

'How old is Buchanan, about fifty? I guess if anything happened to him she'd inherit all his loot.'

'Why, you plannin' on marryin' her?'

The preposterousness of this idea made me give a hoot of laughter. 'Maybe that isn't such a bad idea!'

'You'd probably give him a heart attack iffen you did!'

'So, what else has been happening in this great territory of ours?'

'Crook's been posted north to fight the Sioux up in Wyoming. Traders didn't like him giving that fertile land at Camp Verde to the 'pache, his plan to turn 'em into farmers, with a guaranteed market. The Chiricahua tribe's been moved to that miserable stretch of barren ground along the San Carlos. There's gonna be trouble.'

'No doubt Buchanan was behind that, him and his ring, with their senator in Washington. If a general can't fight him I wonder what chance I got? I suppose all that good work the general did pacifying the tribes has been wasted?'

'Yup. There's chaos now. They're starvin', sullen and angry. There's a nephew of Cochise been stirrin' up the young bucks. Don't know what his Injun name is but the greasers call him Jerome, or Geronimo. Him an' a bunch of 'em broke out from the San Carlos an' headed for the hills. They been burning *ranchos* along the border. The army reckon they got 'em bottled up in the Superstitions, but they'll slip through the net when they want to.'

Sam grabbed at his shotgun, looked fearfully out into the dark, and hastily took another swig.

'Don't worry,' I grinned. 'The 'pache stick in their wicki-ups at night. They're too scared of ghosts and demons in the darkness.'

'Don't be so sure,' Sam said.

This news had spooked me, too, I had to admit it. We had thought when Cochise surrendered that the years-long war with the tribes, the raping, killing, burning and torturing, was at an end. Now it looked like it all might flare up again. Thanks, once more, to Buchanan and his kind. If ever a man needed an arrow in him . . .

'Looks like I was safer back in prison,' I said, and rolled up in the blanket to sleep. 'Soon as I get some cash I better buy me a rifle and revolvers. That ole scattergun of yourn ain't much use. You never know when those boys gonna pop up outa the cactus.' The thought sent a chill through me.

5

We didn't see any sign of trouble, though, as we put the mules to a mile-eating trot over the next days, weaving our way through the ocotillos and dipping down through the smoke trees in the washes. Back on the flats I pulled my bandanna high as I saw dust devils spinning towards us. Dirt kicked up by eighty hooves was already enough to choke a man. Sam rode in the back wagon as brakeman with the remains of his bottle of whiskey to comfort him. We were making good time and he was happy.

'You know,' he said one night as we camped out. 'You got the makings of a good 'skinner the way you handle my babies. An expert teamster's hard to come by. I gotta take this durn mine machinery on to Tombstone after Tucson. Mebbe I kin git you employed as my pardner. The money ain't so bad. There'd be a hundred dollars in your pocket end of the run.'

'I dunno, Sam. It's tempting. I guess I'm gonna need some kinda job 'til I get on my feet again. But — '

'But you're thinkin' of gittin' quits with Buchanan? Or maybe some git-rich-quick scheme like that one you did, hidin' that silver bullion away?'

'Listen, you drunken ole galoot.' I reached out and caught him by his grey beard. 'Don't you ever say that again.'

'OK, OK.' His eyes bulged. 'No need to get het up.'

'Ach!' I released him. 'What's the good? *You* don't even believe me.'

'Waal, I dunno.' He eased his pulled beard. 'There may be somethun' in what you say. I remember once I was deliverin' flour to the Camp Verde Reservation. Least, it was s'posed to be flour. But them sacks seemed durn heavy. When I looked inside the sacks was full of rocks. Maybe Buchanan ain' as honest as he ought to be.'

I gave a scoffing laugh. 'Tell me somethun' new, Sam. I coulda used you as one of my witnesses. The man's a crook, I tell you.'

★ ★ ★

'Mu-ule train! Hagh!' I cracked Sam's black snake over their backs, not to cut 'em up, just to encourage them, and we wheeled on nice and easy with our heavy iron loads, on towards Tucson, the sentinels of the Pichacho Peak and Chief Butte appearing out of the heat haze rising from the flatland. On we went through the cool of their shadow. Occasionally, we called in at stage stations and wells to water the mules.

There had been a sudden downpour out of nowhere and the desert had come alive with poppies and paintbrush, a carpet of colourful flowers, even the vicious clawed cactii, and the tall, fluted saguaros, giving forth blossoms.

We began to meet traffic, ranch buckboards, creaking Mexican *carretas*, army columns pulling howitzers, so we had to pull off the trail to give them room.

Sam took control of the mules as we descended to the mile-wide bottomlands where Tucson lay, shouting out to me when to brake the wheels. If I had been in a normal frame of mind it would have been a wondrous sight, this encirclement of mountains about us, the blue cardboard cut-outs of the Santa Catalinas, the Baboquivari Peak, the Picacho del Alamo Muerte, the Santa Ritas and, seventy-five miles away, the Sierra de la Estrella and the Superstitions where hostile Apaches skulked. But I wasn't in a normal frame of mind. I was brooding on Frank Buchanan. It was like a wound festering away inside of me. I needed revenge.

In five years, Tucson had changed. There were farms of grain, orchards, melons and maize, among the willows

52

and cottonwoods, that had not been there before. Five years of peace had done wonders for those lucky enough to live outside of Yuma's walls. In the town itself, the old Spanish adobes were still there surrounding the wide plazas, with their barred open windows and steerhides for doors. But some fancy new homes had gone up with flowery patios behind high walls. There was a new bank, a big hotel, and numerous stores behind false fronts that had not been there before. Main Street was a bustle of freights, buggies, hitched broncs and *burros*, folk hurrying back and forth. Tucson had prospered while I was away.

Sam took a turn out of Meyer Street into Main Street and I watched with admiration as the mules stepped neatly over the chain and back again as we straightened up, and the way Sam manoeuvred through the throng, yelling at the top of his lungs for folks to watch out.

We eased into the freight livery yard

and I clamped the brake of the back-wagon and jumped down, brushing the dust from my clothes with my hat.

'Yee-hoo!' Sam yelled. 'We made it, pardner.'

A pasty-faced clerk in an apron, shirt sleeves and bowler, came out of the office with a sheaf of bills and pencil in his hand. He gave me a look, and a double-take of slow recognition, of distaste mingled with fear. A look I was going to have to get used to. And I recognized him. He had been on the jury.

'What's he doing here?' he snapped out.

'Meet my new swamper,' Sam yelled.

'Your what?'

'He's a good man. He can do the work. He's bin a godsend. You owe him ten days' wages.'

'No way we do. Nobody told you to take this man on. Where's your regular swamper?'

'He's gawn. I wouldn't have got here without Flynn. I don't care what he might have done.'

'You forget who owns this outfit? There's no way Mr Buchanan's going to have this man working for us.'

'What about my ten days' pay?' I butted in.

'Go ask the birds. We don't employ convicts and bums.'

My temper snapped. I had the fat little slug by the throat and up against the side of the wagon, holding him in the air as he kicked and choked. My fist was raised to smash him, but Sam hung on to me. 'Leave him go, you fool!'

The clerk dropped to the ground, and backed away, feeling his throat, spluttering and pointing an accusing finger. 'You — you can't treat me like this. Get out of my yard. You'll pay. You'll never work in Tucson. Mister Buchanan will see to that.'

I made a move towards him and he turned, hurried back to his office, his arse wobbling in his striped pants.

'You idjit. What you doin'? You could git me the sack. You wanna be thrown back in Yuma? If I weren't here you'd have choked the life outa him.'

'I wish I had,' I spat out. 'So long, Sam.'

'Hey,' he called, plaintively, after me. 'Maybe I — '

I didn't want to hear. My heart was still pounding with anger. Along the street I stripped off my shirt, dunked my head and shoulders into a horse trough. I wanted to cool off. I ran my fingers through my prison crop, put my hat back on. My shirt stank. It hadn't been washed for five years. I put it on again. My belly rumbled with hunger. I sniffed the appetising scent of frying *enchiladas* wafting through the bead door of a *cantina*. I couldn't afford to waste any of my dollars on fripperies. I tightened my belt and walked along in the shade of the canopied sidewalk marvelling at the strangeness of things I hadn't seen for years, rings and watches in a jeweller's window, the array of hardware in a gunsmith's, fat cigars in a tobacco store, fancy shirts in a clothing emporium, all the things I couldn't afford. I even marvelled at the frothy dresses on the dummies, the newfangled bustles and ostrich-feathered hats in a ladies' outfitters. I stared at the men, women and children passing in the street. I felt like I had arrived from another planet. The noise and clamour almost frightened me. And they stared at me, curiously, stepped out of my way. They were all thinking the same thing: watch out for Flynn. He's a convict, a bum. It was true, I was.

6

A new saloon had been built since I was there: The Silver Garter, a spacious two-storey place. I peered over the batwing doors, my dry throat longing for a beer. Suddenly there was a whooping as a curly-haired cowboy came galloping his mustang down the street — 'Hee-yaugh! Hai-yee-hoo!' He scrambled from the saddle on to the sidewalk and burst through the doors into the saloon. He was followed at a more leisurely pace by two horsemen. One was a sullen, leathery, older man, hung with iron. The other was a sallow-skinned dude dressed in silver and black, fringed silk shirt, tight black pants tucked into silver-toed riding boots, cruel rowels on his heels. A straw sombrero shaded his face but I could see his eyes swivel from side to side, checking everyone he saw.

The way he stepped down from his $200 black stallion and hitched him to the rail, the way his hands hovered over the silver-engraved revolvers slung low on his hips, told me he was no ordinary cowpoke. He eyed me, briefly, and sauntered into the saloon. My heart gave an extra thud when I saw the brand on their horses: the Casa Grande!

There were two bottles of whiskey on the bar before them when I followed them in. Curly, as they called him, spat away a cork and tipped his back, his Adam's apple bouncing up and down as he took several good swallows and gasped, 'Whoo!' He was here to have fun. The man in black tipped his bottle more carefully to fill glasses for himself and his companion. Without removing his gloves he put his to his lips and savoured it.

'Howdy.' I nodded at them, friendly-like, and called for a glass of beer. Foam-topped, it came skimming along the copper-covered bar to my waiting hand. Thirstily, I downed half of it in one swallow. I wiped my mouth on the back of my hand. 'You boys from the Casa Grande?'

'What's that to you?' The older man's muddy eyes glimmered viciously. 'Who the hell asked you to butt in?'

'Nobody,' I shrugged. 'How's Buchanan treating you?'

'You know him?' There was a glimmer of humour in the depths of the dude's brown eyes, but they also contained a malign challenge as they met mine. I figured he had some mixed blood in him, although the flat planes of his face were not red-hued like a Mex or Indian, but strangely colourless, his eyes hooded and his jaws swarthy. 'You claiming to be some kind of friend of his?'

I admired the shimmer of the German beer up against the light. 'Golden as heaven.' I let the rest of it slide down my throat before answering. 'Me and him crossed paths five years ago.'

'That a fact?' The dude was about my height, five eleven. He took off his Stetson to reveal a head of greasy curls. He stuck out his chest and spoke, coldly. 'What's the handle?'

'Sean Flynn.' I spoke in a loud clear voice and saw several groups of men at the card tables pause like somebody had jabbed them in the backs and turn to give me the once over. Yes, I was sure getting used to that look. 'Give him my regards.'

'I'll do that,' the black-clothed *hombre* muttered.

He was one of those men whom women might, conceivably, find exciting. He had an air of swagger and menace. Some seemed to fall for those guys, the ones with danger written all over them. And he wasn't short of cash. He tossed down a clatter of silver dollars to pay for his pals.

It was siesta time and the saloon was quiet, just the men playing cards, and a couple of floozies, their painted faces limp with perspiration, sprawled

61

on a horsehair sofa at the far end. One had her knees up, showing her yellow stockings and frilled pantalettes beneath her skirt, but she wasn't drawing much attention. She lit a cigarette and eyed us like a rattler planning when to make her strike. The only sounds were the creaking of a fan on the ceiling pumped by a Mex kid, the murmur of the men, and the flippering of an ivory ball around the spinning roulette wheel. 'Place your bets, gents,' the dealer called. But he hadn't many takers and sounded bored.

The mean-looking cuss was in dusty range clothes, two belts of bullets around his gut, and the well-used walnut butt of a .45 sticking from his holster. He looked like he wouldn't have much hesitation in using it. He pondered me over the rim of his glass as if my name rang a bell.

'Ain't you that lousy punk with a tin badge who came riding into Mister Buchanan's place?' he suddenly said.

'The one who thought he could send him down?'

'That's me,' I gritted out.

'Instead, this stinkin', so-called marshal here got five years in Yuma.' The gunman guffawed, showing his tobacco-stained teeth, and gave the dude a nudge. 'Serve the polecat right, eh, Estevan?'

Estevan's teeth were, at least, a healthier white when he smiled. 'Anybody who takes on Buchanan should be ready for what he gets.'

'This stupid bum!' The ugly pug was killing himself laughing, jerking a thumb contemptuously back my way. I guess he thought that as I had no gun, and looked and smelt like a skunk, I would have to take his taunts. 'This bum thought he could — '

I smiled and signalled to the barman to give me another beer. He sent it sliding to my hand. I picked it up and poured it over the pug's greasy head. He turned, spluttering his amazement. I smashed my left fist into his face, all my frustration of five wasted years powering out through me, all my hatred for his type. I didn't give him a chance to grab his gun. I juddered my right into his kidney, and followed up with a flurry of jarring blows to his head and body. He was one tough *hombre* and didn't go down, so I caught him by his shirt front, gave a quick twist and sent him slithering along the floor. He grunted, shook his head and got back to his knees. My boot heel hit him in the nose and he toppled back. He tried to get to his feet again and I rabbit-punched him with the heel of my palm across the side of his throat. Three more swift kicks finished him. I hauled him up by the scruff of his neck and pants, ran him at the swing doors and tossed him out to the street.

His two *compadres* could have jumped me, or shot me, so I turned ready to take them on, too. But they didn't make a move. Nor did any of the men at the tables. They watched, frozen with surprise.

'You can tell Buchanan that's what he'll get' — I was breathing hard — 'if we ever meet again. And anybody else wants to make any funny remarks.'

Estevan's lip curled back in a slow mocking smile. 'I'll pass the message on.'

'Yeah, me, too,' Curly grinned. 'You sure know how to handle yourself. Here, pal, let me buy you that beer you spilled over poor ole Spike.'

I eased my knuckles as I returned to the bar. Estevan leaned over and felt my biceps beneath my shirt. 'Solid as stone,' he drawled.

'That's what you get,' I said, downing the beer, 'from breaking rocks all day. You should try it sometime.'

'I like your style. But if you go on like that you ain't gonna live long.' The dark-clothed man turned his back to the bar, bracing his elbows on it. Suddenly my glass shattered. Estevan stepped to one side, pulling his silver Sidewinder like lightning. The explosion rocked my ears as he fired, narrowly missing me. I turned to see his bloody-nosed friend standing in the doorway, hanging on to his seared knuckles as his revolver slowly fell from his hand, clattering to the floor.

'That wouldn't be fair, Spike,' Estevan whispered, as the acrid black powdersmoke drifted. 'He ain't wearing a gun.'

'You — ' Spike grimaced with pain, sucking at his knuckles where the bullet had creased the gun from his grasp. 'Whose side you on? Look what he done to my dose.'

'Get back to the ranch,' Estevan spat out. 'I came here for a quiet game of cards, not this tomfoolery. It's too hot.'

Spike grumbled, picked up his revolver, snarled at me, 'I'll be looking for you,' and skulked off into the sunshine.

'Some fancy shooting,' I said. 'Thanks.'

Estevan made a downturned grimace. 'I never did like back-shooters. I like to face a man before I gun him down.

And, anyway, Buchanan might want *me* to kill you. So, he would be doing me out of a thousand dollars.'

'That what you charge?' I muttered, taking a swig of the beer.

'*Si*. Buchanan he pays well to the right man. Maybe you should consider calling off this feud and working for him? Then I would not have to kill you.'

'You'd be well advised, *amigo*,' Curly put in. 'You're lucky Spike's a lousy shot. Next time it won't just be your glass.'

'No, I'm not working for Buchanan. I'm working to get him. You can tell him that.'

'In that case you had better get yourself some protection, my friend. At least a gun. In the meantime, you looking for some other kind of action? Like poker?'

I remembered the miserable few coins left in my pocket and hesitated. 'No, not today. I ain't — '

'Come on.' Estevan gave me a flicker

of a wink. 'We can take these boys.' He wandered over to a group of men. 'Anybody want to join a game?'

'Sure.' A couple of them drew up chairs, relieved that the shooting was over and they weren't included. 'What's it to be?'

'Count me out.' Curly hitched up his gunbelt. 'I got more int'restin' things to do.' He headed, bowlegged, in his flapping chaps, down the room towards the girls. He picked one up and whirled her around. 'Whoo-wee!' He clambered with her in his arms off up the stairs to the rooms.

'He just cain't wait, can he?' The gunslinger in black smiled and took a chair, his back to the wall. 'Stud poker?'

'Suits me.'

He began to deal from a pack as three other fellows joined us. We didn't talk a lot more. Spike was forgotten. I needed to concentrate. It seemed to me the rules had changed while I was inside. The simple plainsman's game of 'bluff' had been complicated. Some mathematical genius had worked out the tables of possibilities and probabilities, and some joker called Hoyle had brought out a compendium of rules. Science had replaced guesswork. Words were passing back and forth like 'aces high', 'stand patter', 'square deal', 'pass the buck', 'showdown'. Estevan, opposite, was as expert with cards as he was with guns. And as cool. I felt out of my depth as, surprisingly, my winnings went up to fifty dollars. I had the uneasy feeling he was letting me win. After three hours I was a hundred dollars to the good. I should have pulled out then, but my credo had always been 'double or nothing'.

Estevan passed his bottle of whiskey round the table. I guessed he must be half-Mexican. He had the elegant manners of the Latinos. But there was an arrogance about him, and contempt in his hooded eyes as if he considered us all fools. An hour later I had lost the lot, apart from a dollar.

'I'm through, gents.' I got to my feet. 'I need this for a beer.'

'You shoulda quit earlier.' Estevan reached out a hand to draw his winnings in. 'I gotta be on my way, too.' He called for Curly and they sauntered out of the saloon. I watched them head out on their broncs the way they had come.

'Well,' I muttered, as I climbed on to a bar stool. 'Now I'm really in the mire.'

It was nearly dusk and the saloon was livening up. More girls had come down from the upstairs rooms to mingle with the men, and a Mex lady had started rippling melodies on a harp in the corner. The roulette wheel was spinning busily. And I had enough for two beers. One of which had half gone. How stupid could a man be?

'Meester Flynn?'

A Spanish girl had climbed on to the bar-stool beside me. She wore a silk dress in passionate flame red and orange, which showed most of her slim brown shoulders and bosom, and from which her bare legs protruded. A dancer's legs of which a man could only dream. Her face — high Spanish cheekbones, black cannibal eyes, blue-black swirl of hair — I had known, but couldn't place.

'I know you?'

'You help me when my father killed. You find me home with Meesis Hanniford.'

'Mercedes?'

'*Si*. You out of jail, Meester Flynn?'

'It would appear so. Jesus, you've changed!' I glanced at her long legs dangling from the stool. 'For the better.'

Her smile flashed, warmly, but there was something puzzlingly cheap about her. 'What you doin'?' I asked, näively. 'Gal like you shouldn't be in here.'

She laughed, tossing her glistening hair out of her eyes. 'You allus did give me the lecture. I work here.'

'You work here?'

'*Si.*' She opened her palms to the ceiling. 'Mercedes. She is the main attraction.'

'You mean you sing?'

'Sure.' She laughed, shrugged her shoulders. 'I sing, I dance, I do anything you wish.'

'You don't say,' I said, getting the picture. 'That ain't good news, Mercedes. What would your mother think?'

'My mother dead. You know that. So is Meesis Hanniford.' She crossed herself twice. 'What else I do? Scrub white folks' floors? Serve table? Wash clothes?'

'It's honest work.'

'So this is honest. Men pay me. I give.'

'Yuk. You mean these fat greasy slobs?'

'Some of them ain' so bad.' She made a grimace. 'Some of them, ya! I would like to keel. But they pay good.'

'It ain't good, Mercedes. It ain't

good for your soul.'

'You a preacher now, Meester Flynn?'

'Call me Sean.' I looked at her lithe brown body. The sleeves of her flared dress hung down to near her elbows. I wanted to pull it down from her, see her naked, same as these men did. I was no different. 'Waal,' I said, bitterly, 'you're wastin' your time with me, gal. I'm broke.'

'I know. I bin watchin' you from the balcony. You sure play bad.'

I leaned forward and sipped my beer. 'I cain't even buy you a drink.'

'I buy you one.' She smiled and signalled to the barkeep. 'Another beer for Meester Flynn, Charlie.'

'Thanks.' I sat there glumly. 'Looks like I'll be sleeping out on the plaza with the other bums.'

'You no need to do that.' She smiled at me, cheekily. 'You come back here one o'clock, two o'clock, maybe. I'll sneak you in. I got a nice bed. Plenty of room.'

'You can do that?'

'Sure, I can have who I like. It my own time.'

'Well, what a surprise. You sure have changed, gal.'

She put an arm around my neck, leaned forward, kissed my unshaven jaw. 'Pooh!' She recoiled. 'You steenk like skunk. You go have bath, buy yourself new clothes.'

'Sure, what with?'

Mercedes took a roll of bills from out of her bodice, peeled off four five-dollar notes, slipped them along the bar to me. 'Go on. Take them. You have a bath or I no let you in.'

'I don't want your money.'

'Call it loan.'

'OK. It's a deal.' I squeezed her hand as I got off the stool. 'Tomorrow I'll get a job.'

'*Mañana*,' she smiled, impishly. 'Always *mañana*. You no forget tonight, Sean.'

7

A tall man, a shotgun under his arm, moved out of the shadows. 'I've been looking for you,' he said. There was a badge gleaming on his chest, the badge I had once worn. 'You only been here coupla hours and already I had complaints.'

'Howdy, Ned. I was going to call on you in the morning. I was wondering if there's any chance you need a deputy?'

'Come on, Sean,' he drawled. 'I've had a complaint from Albert Green in Buchanan's livery yard that you assaulted him. And the doc tells me he treated one of Buchanan's boys, Spike Stephens, for what appears to be a broken nose and abrasions. He claims you beat him up. What you gonna do, go through all Buchanan's men 'til you get to him? This ain't like you, kicking and throttling, getting into brawls for no reason.'

'No reason? I just saw red. The way they spoke to me. I don't have to take insults from anyone. I'm on a hair trigger, Ned. They'll have to learn to stay out of my way. Anyway, I only picked up that li'l squirt Green by his shirt front and give him a shake.'

'He says you tried to throttle him.'

'Aw, I learned to fight dirty in the pen. A case of having to. And that other bastard took a shot at me. You can ask in the saloon.'

'I'm keeping the lid down on this town, Sean. I don't need you to come blowing things up. You gotta see my position. I oughta take you in. I don't want to do that. You go on this way you'll be back in Yuma before you know what's hit you. Unless Buchanan gets to you first.'

'I'll never go back to Yuma, Ned. I'd rather die. You saying that there ain't no job for me? That all those years I gave serving this community counts for nothing?'

'Be reasonable, Sean. There's no way the judge and magistrates gonna reinstate you. They've already made that clear to me. You've got a record.'

Ned was tall, but gangly with it. He was a good man. A family man. He walked a straight line. But I knew he had to keep in with those who ran this territory if he wanted to hang on to his marshal's job. His slow drawl, as we stood on the corner of Meyer Street and listened to the laughter, the tinkle of piano coming from the saloons, was friendly, but also authoritative. He had grown up while I had been gone. He was looking after his town.

'I've got a record for something I didn't do. You know that. Hell, I was a good marshal. You know that, too. It was my life, my career. It was what I always wanted to be. Do you mean that's all blown away? Chrissakes, Ned, I'm twenty-nine. What am I supposed to do? Start a new life?'

'That might not be a bad idea. Go someplace else, Mistuh Flynn. You shouldn't have come back here. You're looking for trouble and that's bad. I don't like the thought of you crossing the line.'

'Don't worry, Ned,' I laughed. 'I ain't gonna rob the bank. At least, not yet.'

'Well, just cool your temper and keep outa trouble. This is an official warning. I used to respect you, Mistuh Flynn. I'd like to think I still can do.'

'What's with the *mistuh* business? I ain't your boss any more.'

'Look, you show me you're straight, maybe, just maybe, I can get the judge to agree to you working for me, or with me, as a special investigator, an undercover man. I've already broached the subject. He knows you're a digger.'

'Yeah? What kinda pay?'

'That we'd have to discuss. I think it's a good idea. I want to give you a chance. I hate to see you in the gutter. Don't let your bitterness get the better of you, Sean. Forget Buchanan.'

'Yeah. What happened to those files on him?'

Ned looked uncomfortable. 'We had a fire. They all got destroyed. Forget it, Mistuh Flynn. The case is closed on him.'

'Yes. It would be.'

Ned started to move away. 'Come over an' have supper with Mary an' the boys one night, will ya?' he called back.

'Sure,' I said.

* * *

A hot tub in the bath-house, a shave, and clean shirt and socks made me feel a lot less sore at the world. And a big meal in a Mexican *cantina* helped. There was a starter that looked like a dead frog but turned out to be cactus (with its spikes burned off) in red pepper sauce, onions and garlic. Hot as hell. I cooled my tongue with a bottle of red, and a goat's cheese salad of tomatoes and olives with new baked bread. The main course was chopped pork coated with honey, with red chillis and blackeye beans. It made a change to prison fare. A glass of tequila and a five-cent cigar gave the finishing touch. Suddenly I felt human again.

I hung around until late before making my way back to The Silver Garter. I stood outside and listened to screams of laughter emanating from the upstairs windows. I didn't like to think what Mercedes and the other gals were doing up there. I was nervous as a bobcat. Any man who hadn't had the touch of a woman for five years would be. Gradually the saloon emptied, the last customers swaggering away into the night.

Mercedes stuck her head out of the door. 'Come on in,' she called. 'What you doin' out there?'

The other girls were having a late supper over in the corner and there were a lot of curious glances, nudges and giggles, as Mercedes took me upstairs. I had had a long day and

I was dog-tired, and the wine, whiskey and tequila didn't help, not to mention the beers, but I knew I wasn't going to get much sleep.

Mercedes was beautiful, real beautiful, as she stripped naked in the lamplight and climbed into bed with me. I wanted her, wanted her more than any girl I'd ever known. At first it was good, we were wild and desperate for each other, kissing and clutching at each other. And then something in my mind snapped. Maybe it was the thought of her and all those other men in this soiled bed? Maybe . . . I wanted to, but I just couldn't do it. God, how I wanted to!

'Don' worry,' she whispered, her fingers soothing me. 'I heard 'bout this. Men been in jail long time they . . . they need time, they gotta relax.'

'I ain't men. I'm me,' I said, raising myself on my shoulders and staring at her.

'You wait, *mi amor*, one day it will be good between us. I wait long time for you. I can wait leetle longer.'

I rolled away from her, clung to the edge of the bed, stared into my future. What the hell was happening to me?

* * *

In the morning I got out early while she was still sleeping. I felt bad, humiliated. This had never happened to me before. I went down to Jose Ochoa's corrals. Perhaps he needed a bronc-buster? No, he'd got a good man. Instead I shifted horse manure in his stables for five hours, piling it on to carts to be sent out to the farms. The flies buzzed, the sweat rolled from me. The labours of Hercules, or whoever it was, for fifty cents an hour. At noon I tossed my shovel away with contempt. Was this what I had become? Was this what was left to me?

The nights didn't improve none. Mercedes never complained. She clung on to me in that narrow bed and was soon blissfully asleep. Let's face it, she didn't really need me. Maybe she was glad to find a man who *didn't* do it. But it didn't do a lot for my temper. I began drinking more and more, getting into card games I couldn't win. I tried for other jobs, stage-driver, bank security man, even store-keeper. None wanted me. They gave me that funny look. The crooked marshal. The man with a record. I considered trying silver prospecting along at Tombstone, but most of the big seams were already played out, the mines flooded. I could have offered my services to the army as a scout, but why get a poisoned arrow in my rump for the peanuts they paid?

Mercedes left money out for me on her table each morning. It was dirty money. But it was just a loan. I jotted every dollar down in my notebook. One day, I vowed, I would pay her back. Most of it went back into the saloon kitty on whiskey or roulette. It crossed my mind to do what I had joked about to Ned — hit the bank and get out quick. But did I want to become some God-useless badman on the lam, a price on my head, no place to go? No, in my heart, I still hankered for a decent life, a useful place in frontier society. If I was to settle with Buchanan the best way would be to do it legally. Or, at least, as legal as possible.

One night decided me. A surly, bearded farmer had had a big win at roulette and was in the mood to spend. Mercedes screamed as he grappled with her, tore her dress. I was on my feet and spun him round, my fist raised.

'Whassa matter, mistuh?' he guffawed, already pie-eyed. 'I allus wanted the highest-priced gal in the house and tonight I'm gonna have her.'

'Don't, Sean! It don' matter.' Mercedes hooked her slim arm around the farmer's burly neck, her pert breasts protruding from her torn dress. She gave me a slight wink. 'He buy me new dress. He buy me lots of theengs. Won' you honey?'

'Aw, don't worry about him,' a voice

in the crowd called. 'He's just a pimp, a lush, a no-good jailbird. The famous ex-marshal.'

I spun around to see who had spoken, but I was well whiskied-up, myself, and there was just a haze of grinning faces. It was true, wasn't it? I ignored the jeers and headed for the door. There, I turned and looked back. Mercedes, her eyes lustrous, was laughing as she hauled the beefy farmer up the staircase. She looked so heart-breakingly wanton . . .

It was time to take control of my life.

★ ★ ★

It was a warm night and I slept out on the dusty plaza among the waggoners and their teams of mules. Some had come up from south of the border, but most of the rigs bore the name 'Buchanan'. I couldn't get away from that man. In the morning I bought myself a ten-dollar mustang, a cheap saddle, a bedroll, a few supplies, and a leather gunbelt with secondhand revolver from the pawnshop. I stacked the belt with bullets, vowed to give up the whiskey and poker and get out into the wide open spaces that I loved.

Old Sam was staggering along Tucson's dusty main street hanging on to the neck of his white mule, Esmeralda. She was managing to hold him up. He certainly served as a warning to any man to stay off the booze. 'You hung another one on?' I asked, reining in.

'They fired me. All these years of service an' that li'l runt Albert Green had me booted outa the yard.' Sam waved an empty whiskey bottle at me, forlornly. 'What am I s'posed to do now?'

'What you doin' with that mule? Don't she belong to the Buchanan company?'

'Nope, she don't.' Sam lurched forward and tried to give the mule a kiss on the nose. 'Esmeralda's my sweetheart, my personal property. Not another lead mule like her in the whole of Arizon-ey.' I expected the beast to bite for she had drawn back her lips to expose her teeth. Instead, she flickered her tongue to give him a wet wash and uttered a massive bray. 'Hear that? Esmeralda says she's allus gonna be mine.'

'Waal, a gal cain't be choosy these days. I guess she don't notice your breath.'

'Who's her daddy's li'l gal?' he warbled, fondling her ears. 'Best jerkline mule ever been, aincha? An' they don' wancha?'

'That so?' Sam had given me an idea. He was tipping up the bottle, waggling his tongue to scoop the last dregs. 'You want to work for me?'

'Heck! How kin I work for you, Mistuh ex-lawman?'

'I'm gonna buy you two beers. That's all. You drink 'em slow. Sober up.' I dismounted outside The Silver Garter and led him inside. 'I'll see you in a little while.'

I climbed the stairs to the rooms and found Mercedes still in bed, naked beneath the sheet. The farmer had gone, minus most of his money. Mercedes grinned and produced a handful of greenbacks from beneath the pillow. 'Look what he geev me!'

'Yeah, and what did you have to give him?'

'That nuthin',' she shrugged. 'Don't be jealous, Sean.'

'How can I help it. You're sending me crazy. I'm leaving you, Mercedes.'

'Leaving me? Why you leave me?' She looked startled, her shining black hair tumbled across her face as she propped herself on one elbow. 'You cannot leave me, *mi corazon*. I need you. You need me.'

'No, I've got to get away, be on my own for a while. You know your father's place, the farm? I thought, maybe, I'd go out there, get it operational again.'

'Sure, why not? It still there, the *casa*

the land. You can have it, Sean. Or run it for me. But, farming no good. You break your back for what? For Buchanan to take his cut.'

'Buchanan?'

'*Si*, all along the valley the Mex farmers they have to pay him protection.'

'Protection money? That's daylight robbery.'

'*Si*, but what can we do? His men come down from the hills, say we must pay. They have guns. We not. And then we must use his haulage firm to move our produce up to the markets at Flagstaff or Phoenix. He charge way over top. Pah! What's the use?'

'Ain't there no alternative? No other haulier?'

'No. The alternative? Stay poor. Or get shot. Buchanan, he want the cream.'

'I'd heard about this, but I didn't know it was so bad. We're going to have to stop him. There is an alternative. You and me.'

'Oh, yes,' she laughed. 'How's that?'

'Mercedes, how much cash you got? You told me you'd got some saved.'

She looked startled for a moment. 'Under the bed or in the bank?'

'Both. I want you to sponsor me. Make me a loan.'

Her brow furrowed as she hesitated. 'You want me to geev you all my money?'

'Not give. I'll pay you back with interest.'

'Hmm?' She touched her lips and lowered her voice. 'Don' tell nobody. I done good. Men, they crazy, they geev me much money. An' Meesis Hanniford, she leave me leetle bit. I guess I got near two t'ousand dollar.'

'That much?' I gave a whistle of surprise. 'That's enough to get a team and wagon together. Mercedes, how'd you like to loan it to me? Or be my partner?'

'Partner?' She crossed her eyes with a little girl look, puffed her hair out of her eyes. 'That sounds good.'

'We're going into business. We'll set

up in opposition. We'll give Buchanan and his boys a run for his money.'

'Sean, be careful.' She reached out her arms, trying to draw me into bed with her. 'You sure you can do this?'

'I can try.' I knelt, hugging her, her musky hair touching my face as I kissed her warm, wet lips. 'I'm gonna deliver your Mexican *amigos'* produce to market for a fair price.'

'Sean!' She gave a theatrical sob. 'You theenk I like this life?'

'No?' I smiled. 'You could have fooled me.'

'Soon I geev up this bad life. I promise you. We will be married in church before God. Then, I hope to Jesus, you will really want me.'

'I will always want you,' I whispered to her. 'But not like this. So long, partner.'

'Wait,' she said, stretching. 'I go over to bank. Get you money. All you want.' She smiled as if it was all settled. 'When we marry I come an' live at *casa* with you. We have lots of babies.'

'Mmm? Maybe.' I detached her fingers that were lingering about my loins. 'Maybe then I'll be able to rise to the occasion. Here's your dress. Go hit the bank, *muchacha*.'

★ ★ ★

Mercedes was as good as her word and came back with an envelope stuffed with cash. While she was away I told Sam, 'We're gonna need a good wagon and nineteen mules. We'll go down to Ochoa's yard see what he's got. You're going to be my first driver. I'll act as swamper and guard. I need you to teach me all you know.'

The old-timer hooted with glee. 'Esmeralda's the one. She'll teach ya. She'll teach them other mules. All you gotta do is keep me in whiskey.'

'No. I'll pay now for your meals for a week in the saloon. No booze. You can sleep in the wagon. When you've got the rig ready you bring it out to

Jaime Ostos' old place. We'll make that our freight yard. You're gonna have to earn your next bottle.'

Mercedes walked along with us to the corrals where Sam, with a lot of umming and aahing, looked at the teeth and hooves of the available mules. There were a dozen half-decent ones, and Ochoa promised another seven. Then we visited the blacksmith's in the Mexican quarter where I remembered seeing an old freight wagon, lacking a tongue and one wheel, in the back yard. The smithy told us he had run a team of his own until Buchanan had warned him he could well meet with an accident.

'It safer to shoe horses,' he said. 'But I soon feex thees wagon for you, *señor*. It make me happy to see someone take on Buchanan. Maybe I can get you a second trail wagon, too.'

I left Sam sorting out the bits and pieces of harness the Mex had available. I figured now he had an interest he would stay clear of whiskey for a week or so. I kissed Mercedes, climbed on my bronc, and headed out of town. For a total outlay of $1,600 we had the start of a freighting business. Suddenly life looked good.

8

It was good to be back in the saddle, away from the city, jogging along a winding white trail that followed the valley bottom, the landscape a *mélange* of yellows, greens and purples, scattered with grey outcrops of rock, pleasing to the eye. My horse was no great shakes, just a scrubby dun mustang who had been ill-schooled and badly used, but he did his best. I had to keep prodding him with my spurs to keep him at a fast trot. Like all critters he was suffering from the heat of the scorching sun which was soaring high in a clear blue heaven. It was early yet but the temperature was well into the 90°s. My cheap, serviceable carbine was hooked over the saddle horn. I was not expecting trouble, but in this wild country a man had to be always on the lookout.

Mercedes' was one of the first properties I came to. An adobe with a flat roof built on a bed of rocks and set back among its dusty fields. It certainly had a deserted, run-down look. As I climbed up the steps to the front veranda I froze at a rattling sound and an angry hiss. A diamondback was sunning himself in a corner and reared up at my approach, his fangs bared. My carbine was back on the horse, so, instead of blasting him to hell, I stepped cautiously around.

'You stay in your corner, pal,' I crooned to him, 'and we might just get along.'

I pushed open a creaking door into the first of two rooms. The pack rats and termites who lived in the rocks and the roof, had done their best to demolish whatever was in there, but an iron bedstead had been too tough for their teeth. I was going to need a new mattress, that was for sure, and a table and chair. In the backroom there was a stone stove and cooking pots covered with dust and rat shit. Anything edible had been gnawed through. Nothing a good broom and hammer and nails couldn't fix.

Out back, I peered down a fifty-foot well. I lowered a bucket and brought up an insect-strewn specimen of water. The well was going to need cleaning out, the water pump repaired. I gave the water to the horse, who supped it, gratefully. The fields all about were covered in weeds, the fences broken. Her father must have nigh broken his back scratching a living from this dust. It was going to need a lot of work. Who knew, maybe one day I would call it home.

I rode on to take a look at the other farms and maybe get some ideas. Only twenty years before, this whole territory had been part of the Mexican empire, along with New Mexico, a good slice of Texas and all of California. There had been some sort of contretemps and the US had sent a gunboat and marched troops into Mexico City. General Santa

Anna had quickly thrown in the towel and handed over this vast area to the States. Ironically enough, immediately afterwards, gold had been discovered in California and the Fortyniners had dug millions of dollars of the stuff out of the ground. Of course, I'd been too young to get in on the rush. This is by way of explaining that the land is still peopled mainly by 'Mexicans', as if you didn't know.

It was noticeable, however, as I rode, that since my incarceration many of the more fertile stretches of land, with access to the river, had been snapped up by Anglo settlers. The Latinos had been pushed back onto the scrubbier ground. I turned the mustang at a jog trot into one of these farms. It was no more than a scabby collection of shanties, but the fields had been planted with melons and corn, which were ripening in the sun. There was no sign of life, but there was a trickle of woodsmoke from a chimney and a scent of *frijoles* cooking.

There was a battered, wooden-wheeled *carreta* nearby, for a Mexican a sign of prosperity. Not many owned such vehicles. I stepped down, called out, 'Anybody home?' and tapped lightly on a closed door of the main cabin. There was no answer. It was like I could sense people inside holding their breath and hoping I'd go away. I banged some more and yelled out in Spanish that I was their neighbour and *amigo*. Eventually a bolt was released and the door opened a narrow gap. The dark eyes and pitted planes of a man's unshaven face showed.

'Yuh?' There was a sullen fear in his eyes. 'What you want here, *señor*?'

'Just to say how-do. I'm taking over the place of Jaime Ostos. I need to hire some help.'

'You ride for Señor Buchanan?'

That made me smile. 'No. Not me.'

The door was opened and I glimpsed a woman, a couple of other *hombres* and children around a table. The man slipped out and closed the door. 'I got

99

no men to spare. I need them to pick my crop.'

'When's that going to be?'

'Pretty soon. Two week, maybe.'

'You're gonna need someone to haul the crop to market. I've got a wagon and mule team.'

'Señor Buchanan's teamster does that.'

'How much does he charge?'

The farmer made a downturned grimace. 'Six cents a pound.'

'Tell him to get lost. I can do it for two and a half.'

The Mexican shuffled his feet, uncomfortably. 'I don' wan' trouble, meester. I got wife, children.'

'Strike a blow for freedom. You can save money, give them a better life.'

The Mexican stood there in his white cotton garb, rope-soled *huaches*, undecided. 'Two and half. Thass good deal, *señor*. But who will protect me from Buchanan's guns?'

'I will. Come on, he can't just mow us all down.'

'He has many guns. You are only one.' He scratched at himself and spoke, dully. 'My father, when this land become part of the United States, he theenk everything change for us. We got vote in democratic republic. Now we have good life. But nothing much change. We got no chance against the ring.'

'What's your handle?'

'Pablo Velasquez.'

'So, Pablo, you're ready to be a downtrodden second-class citizen the rest of your life? That the world you want your kids to grow up into? Come on, put some fire in your belly. Let's fight him.'

Pablo's fat face split into a grin. '*Señor*, maybe I will save myself some money this year. I let you know when I need you.'

'That's the spirit.' I shook his hand and slapped his shoulder. 'Good man. We'll get your harvest to market, don't worry.'

I jumped onto my bronc, waved

solong, and headed away along the trail to the next farm. But as I did so a cold chill of doubt struck me: what was I getting these *peons* into? Bloodshed was the last thing they wanted.

★ ★ ★

When I rode back into Tucson a few days later I was in a better frame of mind. The sweatiness and shivers that too much whiskey imparts had left me. I had sweated it out putting an old plough of Jaime's to the horse and started on the dust fields. I had marked out plans for new corrals and barns and was feeling pretty optimistic. I rounded the ruined wall out of Church Street into the old part of town and gave a shout of joy when I saw a double-trailer with new tongue and wheels standing in the blacksmith's yard. It was freshly painted in yellow and red like a circus wagon, and on its sides was enscrolled, 'Flynn's Freighters'. Old Sam was busy hooking up Esmeralda and the mules to the jerkline.

'Yay-hoo!' he hollered. 'I was jest about to come lookin' for ya.'

'It's great. You've earned yourself a bottle, oletimer.'

The blacksmith, too, was all smiles, and agreed a reasonable price.

My next stop was the office of the *Arizona Citizen* where I picked up a copy of that day's edition. There on the front page was my box ad: *Flynn's Freighters — Cheapest Rates in the Territory — Deliveries to all Destinations*. That should put Buchanan's nose out of joint for a start.

I called in on the editor, Joe Wesson, and explained my plan to challenge the ring. 'All I want is the peaceful right to work,' I said, 'as laid down in the Constitution.'

'You know what you're doing?' Wesson, in eyeshade and shirt garters, was at his desk looking through proofs. 'Buchanan and the other big operators have got a stranglehold on this territory.'

'If they want to play dirty then I'll operate my Constitutional right to defend myself. With arms, if need be.'

'That's fighting talk.'

'It is. It's war.'

Wesson struck me as an honest man who had done a lot to improve Tucson like getting the town council to install street lights, or clean up the piles of rubbish that were thrown out into the street. Nowadays refuse was regularly carted out of town and thrown down a ravine. It made the town a pleasanter place. He had also backed General Crook's efforts to give the Chiracahua Apaches good land up at Camp Verde, but that had all been blown away by the ring.

'I don't know whether you were set up or not, but as far as I'm concerned, Flynn, you have served your time and I'll give you any support I can,' he told me. 'You're a brave man if you're going to try single-handed to break the monopoly. I only hope I don't have to attend your funeral.'

'I'm not planning on holding it just yet. I'm going to reopen the case against Buchanan. I'm getting new evidence and witnesses. I intend to clear my name. I'll prove that that man's no more than a lousy bandit hiding out in the rocks of Casa Grande.'

'If you come up with hard facts we'll back you. They haven't gagged us yet,' he said. 'Maybe I'll write an article about you for the next edition.' And he started pumping me with questions.

As I left the office, Wesson called out sharply, 'Flynn — be careful!' Not another one worried about my health!

To avoid the temptations of whiskey and poker in The Silver Garter I went into The Hole-in-the-Wall in Gay Street for a beer and some shade during the hot afternoon. Some remarkably attractive 'girls' hovered around the bar. 'Hey, sugar,' one lisped. 'You like a good time?'

'Not with you, honey,' I said, and

took my glass over to a table. I had heard that beneath their paint and their off-the-shoulder ruffled dresses they were Mexican youths. Catamites. No accounting for men's taste. But not my glass of beer. The barman provided me with pen, ink, and paper and I spent my time writing a letter to my brother, Bob, who had a law practice in Santa Fe. Now that I was free I suggested he take my case to appeal. I wrote down all I knew about Buchanan's dirty operations and suggested that we open a private prosecution against the man. I gave him instructions in the event of my death under suspicious circumstance . . .

Bob had always been the serious one out of us two, the swot, who preferred to have his head in a book rather than out playing games or riding horses. He had always advised caution when I had been the hothead. Generally, he was proved right. We had been brought up in Santa Fe, my father fighting for the Stars and Stripes and getting in the way of a cannon shot at the Battle of Glorietta Pass. My mother passed away shortly afterwards from fever, or a broken heart. One thing they had instilled into us was a desire to see justice done. Sometimes I was glad my mother had not lived to see my downfall. In some ways, I wrote, I was doing what I was doing now for her.

'*Adios, muchachas,*' I called to the boy-girls and strolled up to Convent Street to the post office. The Butterfield Overland Stage was about to pull out headed for Santa Fe, so I paid the post and stuffed my letter in the bag. The guard gave a blast on his horn as the coach and four wheeled away in a cloud of dust. There were two youths sprawled in the shade of the sidewalk and we watched it go.

'Got a quarter to spare, buddy?' one of them asked. 'I ain't eaten for days.'

'Maybe you should get up off your butt and find yourself a job.' I glanced at the youth who had spoken. He looked like an Apache by his long black hair hanging to his shoulders from beneath his battered hat, by his cotton pants and moccasin boots. 'Is that you, Chaco?'

'*Si*, it is me,' he replied, sullenly.

I recognized him. He was Mexican by birth but had been captured by the Apaches and brought up by them. When he was eleven he had been taken prisoner by the soldiers in a raid on his people's hideout up above Hell Canyon. Instead of being sent to the reservation he, as a Mexican, had been left to hang around town. He had Apache ways, but not their fierceness. Nonetheless, because of the intense hatred for the Indian he was one of the despised.

'How's it going?'

He shrugged and grimaced. 'You know how. Nobody wants me around. Not easy get job.'

'I had a job.' The blond-cropped youth by his side smiled when he saw me flip a quarter to Chaco. 'But I got fired. I'm hungry, too.'

'Too bad,' I sighed. 'Why'd you get fired?'

'Why, the big boss found me canoodling with his daughter behind the barn. He had his men beat me up and throw me out without a cent. They made a good job of it.'

'Yeah, I was wondering where you got the fat lip and swollen eye. Who'd you work for?'

'Guy called Buchanan up at Casa Grande. His filly sure is a wild thing. Since his wife died he watches her like a hawk. He don't give her much chance to fly. It's almost unhealthy the way he watches over that gal.'

'That so?' I scratched my jaw and considered them. The blond kid was just another drifter, originally from Texas, called Steve. 'You boys interested in farm work? I got plenty needs doing, well-cleaning, roof repairs, fields to be ploughed. But I mean work,

I don't mean no lazing around. No liquor allowed.'

'Yeah? Whadd'ya pay?'

'Thirty dollars a month and your keep. Going rate.'

'Sounds OK,' Steve agreed, and the 'Apache' nodded and got to his feet.

'I should warn you, it might be dangerous. Buchanan is no friend of mine.'

They eyed each other, and nodded again.

'Come on. I'll fit you out with a horse and gun. Meet me back here at sundown ready to hit the trail.'

* * *

In The Silver Garter I bought Sam his bottle and gave Mercedes the good news, but a flicker of worry crossed her brow. 'You sure this wise, Sean?'

'Why, what's wrong?'

'Estevan was in here looking for you. He left you this.' She reached behind the bar and brought out a toy-size hand-made coffin with my name on. 'He say he been hearin' bad things. He tell me to warn you not to go into business. An' not to poke your nose into things don't concern you. Or else.'

I've got to admit the coffin in my hand gave me a nasty start. 'Did you say you bank-rolled me?'

'No, I just say I sold you my land.'

'Good. So there's no need for you to worry. I'll handle Estevan.'

'He's fast, Sean. Like greased lightning. I seen him kill men with hardly a flicker of his eye.'

'Well, he ain't gonna kill me,' I laughed. 'Not if I can help it. We're in business and there's no stopping us.'

'*Nombre de Dios!*' She crossed herself. 'You *gringos*, you all *loco*.'

'Look, I've lost a big hunk of my life. Next year I'll be thirty. I've got a year to prove I can be somebody. You know what they say, if you ain't made it by thirty you're never going to. Don't you want to risk your money?'

'I don' wan' you to reesk your life. Money, I no care about.'

'My life's at risk every day I'm in Tucson, every day that Buchanan runs this town, I'm aware of that, Mercedes. But it's time to fight.'

She flung her arms around me, kissing and sobbing, but I pulled her off. 'I got things to do.' Sure, I knew any moment a sniper's bullet might get me in the back but it was the chance I had to take.

9

It was crimson dusk as I left The Silver Garter and I froze as a voice rang out, 'Are you Sean Flynn?'

My hand automatically went to the butt of my Colt Lightning as I slowly turned to see who wanted me. It was something of a relief to see a tall soldier. He was dressed in the uniform, with red sash, of quartermaster sergeant.

'That's me,' I said.

'Good. I saw your advertisement. The army's got twenty tons of freight needs transporting up to Fort Bowie. Saddles, picks, shovels, nails, wire, kegs of horseshoes, ropes, chains, cases of rifles, Springfields, and assorted ammunition. Can you handle it?'

'Handle it?' I whooped. 'Sure I can. When?'

'Tomorrow. This is an emergency.'

'We'll be there daybreak at the

garrison.' I glanced around and saw Chaco and Steve sitting on a stoop waiting for me. 'Boys,' I shouted. 'We ain't going out to the farm just yet. We've got a job on tomorrow. Go over to the *cantina* and I'll join you for a meal.' I grinned at the sergeant. 'I'll take them along to guard the truck. It's a long haul up into the mountains, but I can guarantee delivery in six days.' Suddenly I regretted giving Sam his whiskey, but said, reassuringly, 'Cheapest rates in the territory.'

'That's what I heard,' the sergeant said, and led me away to sign the agreement. 'No need to worry about the Apache. I'll give you an armed guard of twenty troopers.'

I gave him a grin of grim satisfaction. 'That's fine.' It wasn't the Apache I was worried about. It was Buchanan.

* * *

It wasn't hard to find Sam the next morning. He was snoring lustily among the sprawled drunks on the sidewalks of the saloons sleeping where they had been thrown out the night before. I hauled him up over my shoulder and put a bottle in his paw. His pattern was a two-day binge. He would need another drink as soon as he felt himself getting sober. 'Gorr!' he groaned, pulling the cork out with his teeth. 'Why me?'

I shook my head sorrowfully. 'Self-pity fuelled by whiskey has brought many a man low. It nearly did for me the first weeks back in this city. You gotta pull yourself together, Sam. We got work to do.'

'That man's not driving this wagon, is he?' The quartermaster sergeant was alarmed to see me heave Sam aboard after we had loaded the double-trucks. 'This is a valuable cargo. There's a precipitous trail up ahead.'

'He'll be OK by the time we reach the gradients,' I said. 'You've got my guarantee.'

It would be some while before

we reached the rough, steep and winding trail through the Chiricahuas. That would be when I'd be needing all Sam's expertise and know-how. I was determined to get this first cargo through. Buchanan would have charged five cents a pound, or more. The quartermaster seemed well satisfied with my agreement of two and a half cents. A ton-load added to a thousand dollars. Wow! I had never dreamed there was so much cash to be made. No wonder Buchanan and the other teamsters wanted to keep the trade to themselves. Heavy freight rigs were in short supply and big demand. The railroad had yet to reach these parts. Why, when I'd paid Sam his $150 I'd have almost enough to buy another mule team and trucks. I could see why the teamsters wanted the Apache to keep the army occupied. They were good for business.

Our platoon of soldiers had mounted up, the lieutenant in charge shouted out, 'Get these wagons rolling,' and

I tossed a stone at Esmeralda's rump, making her leap away, cracking my whip over the other babies as they took the strain and we were off. Soon we were out of the town and going at a good pace along the ancient Spanish highway, El Camino Real. Five miles out, however, I saw a line of men drawn up across the trail in a U-circle on their mustangs. They had rifles in their hands and looked like they meant business. I thanked my lucky stars for the presence of the army and shouted out, 'Looks like we got company, Lootenant. You'd better be prepared for trouble.'

He ordered his men to draw their seven-shot Spencers from their saddle holsters and to ease one into the breech. He, himself, rode to the head of our column. As we drew closer I saw Estevan in the centre of his men on his black stallion, and I called to the mules to 'Whoa down'.

'What do you want?' the officer demanded.

'You will have to turn back,' Estevan said. 'This man is not a licensed operator. He has no right to carry this load.'

'You come with me, *hombre*.' The lieutenant led Estevan back to me. 'This man says you're not licensed. Is that so?'

'It's news to me you need a licence to set up in business in Arizona Territory. I'm a former US marshal and I know there's no such statute in the book.'

'He has to have a licence,' Estevan said. 'Issued by the Territorial Teamsters Union. Otherwise he can't get through.'

'Yeah, and who runs the union? Your boss, Buchanan? Tell them to get out of our way, Officer.'

Estevan pointed a finger at me and started to say, 'I warn you — ' but the lieutenant cut him short.

'This is army equipment, mister. We got a war to fight. Maybe you ain't heard? We ain't interested in your squabbles. Get your men off our road or I'll order my troopers to fire.'

If Estevan's face could have paled beneath its tan it would have. He stared at me with cold fury and jerked his stallion around, moving back to his men. 'Yee-haugh!' I yelled, cracking my whip. Unfortunately, accidentally-on-purpose, its lead tip caught Estevan's straw Stetson and cut it from his head. He whirled back at me, his hand going to his revolver, but stopped when he saw the carbines trained on him. 'Gee, sorry,' I said. 'I ain't got the hang of this thang yet.'

Estevan got down to retrieve his hat which was rolling away on the desert breeze. He pointed his gloved finger at me again, 'One of these days!'

'Any time,' I yelled, getting the mules moving. 'Do call on me.'

'If we see you men again on this trail we shoot on sight,' the lieutenant roared. 'Savvy?'

The desperadoes snarled like beaten curs, but moved out of our way, and the troopers kept them covered as we went through. I glanced back and saw the horsemen cantering away back towards Tucson.

'That's settled their hash for a while,' I muttered to Chaco and Steve. 'But I ain't over eager to meet that man in a gunfight. I figure he's a deal faster than me.'

We saw little other sign of life after that just the limitless expanses on either side of dusty desert scrub, the vicious catclaw, cholla and barrel cactus which would tear a rider's legs to shreds unless he were wearing *chaparejos*, and the fluted saguaros, standing like sentinels, their arms raised to the cloudless blue sky. Out there, somewhere, there might be Apache, but if there were we saw no sign of them.

To the south the Santa Ritas lay purple in the distance. Ahead rose the Chiricahuas. Far away across the line in Mexico was the San Ignatio range. We rolled on our way, steadily eating up the miles, across a broad *cienaga* of grass, past the turn off to old Fort Crittenden, on across the desolate treeless plain. We camped out at night under the stars when all the creatures who had been sleeping under rocks during the heat of the day came out to prowl. Sentries were posted all night but there was no real danger of Apaches until dawn.

'You know,' Steve said to Chaco one night as we sat around our fire. 'You'd look a lot less like a durn Injin if you cut your hair. Then folks wouldn't hate you so much.'

Chaco pulled his poncho closer against the night chill and shook his head. 'No way, *compadre*. I cut my hair I lose my strength, my manhood. The Apache very proud of their hair. They always combing it, keep it clean.'

'You don't still believe their mumbo jumbo?' — Chaco was very wary about staying anywhere we could hear the hooting of owls, an evil omen — 'Like not having sex for five days before going on the warpath?'

Chaco grinned. 'I'd be glad to get it any day.'

'I've seen you drinking water through a straw. What's the point of that?'

'That's what they taught me to do. It must not touch the lips.'

'He was with his tribe from the age of five to eleven years,' I put in. 'His formative years. Old habits die hard.'

'If you think like an Apache why don't you go back and join them?'

'Me, no. I don't want to live out in chapparal, chased from pillar to post, shot at on sight. I'm Mex. I like white man's ways.'

We all laughed as a trooper owl-hooted and Chaco's eyes rolled fearfully, anticipating ghosts. 'Don't worry about them teasing you,' I said. 'Let's get some shut-eye.'

The San Pedro crossing was just a trickle of water. The mules drank eagerly. It was hot thirsty work for them. But now the real struggle commenced, the long climb through the Chiricahuas, up to an altitude of 4,800 feet. Sam was sober again and took over the mules. I watched carefully as he manoeuvred the steep gravel bends, our side wheels often only a foot from the cliff edge, yawning space stretching out below. I needed all the driving tips I could get. It was with some relief that I glimpsed the stockade of Fort Bowie amid an ocean of grama grass. 'We've made it!' I yelled.

The gates were opened for us to trundle in on to the wide parade-ground surrounded by rock and adobe buildings on four sides. The soldiers gave us an ironic cheer as we drew in before the office of the captain in command of this 6th Cavalry outpost. He said that they had had a run-in with Apaches the week before and had lost a good man. I was relieved to hear that our platoon would escort us back to Tucson. They had to return, in any case.

'Captain,' I said, 'would you do me a favour — lock up my old swamper, Sam? I'm afraid one of your men might trade him a bottle of hooch. It's for his and our good. We're going to need him on the down grades.'

Old Sam was not amused and cursed mightily as he was led away. But he had a clear head in the morning and we made good time with the empty wagons back to Tucson.

I was in high spirits when the quartermaster handed me an army cheque for a hefty sum and I took Sam and the boys into The Silver Garter to celebrate. Mercedes gave a shrill Spanish screech of joy as I whirled her in my arms and showed her the cheque.

'You can either have part of your cash back now or keep it invested in the company.'

'I leave it with you, Sean. I theenk we goin' be reech.'

'Don't speak too soon,' I said. 'Buchanan's gonna have something to say about that.'

10

'It lookin' good!' Mercedes exclaimed when she rode back with me to the *casa* in the evening. 'You already make big change. One day this gonna be our home. Soon I give up my bad life.'

'That day can't come soon enough as far as I'm concerned,' I said. 'You know that.'

Her face fell and she stared at her shapely sun-bronzed legs. Maybe, it occurred to me, she'd grown too fond of that rip-snortin' life, the music and fun, all those ole boys touchin' and teasin' her, being the centre of attention. Nor, for that matter, was I really interested in being a farmer. My ambition was to clear my name and get back in the saddle with a star pinned on my chest again. A marshal was what I had always wanted to be.

We were sitting on the porch watching

the sunset and Mercedes changed the subject, pointing to the snake coiled in his corner. 'Why you let that nasty ole rattler stay there?'

'Reggie was here first. It's his home same as mine. He used to rear and rattle at me but he's gotten used to me sittin' here quiet-like.'

'He's a funny watchdog.'

'Yep, but a good one. He starts hissin' and rattlin' if anybody steps through this way. He suits me.'

'You crazy man,' she said. 'But, I theenk, good man.'

'I wouldn't be so sure about that. In fact, I haven't told anybody else this, but I am a murderer. I've broken the ultimate law of God and man.'

'Murderer?'

'Yep. I've killed men in the course of my duty when they wouldn't surrender. Most of those rats deserved swift justice. But then I had the backing of man's law. You know that thug who raped you, killed your father? He was in Yuma. I cornered him outside the canteen one night, stuck a spike in his guts, finished him.'

'But, Sean, this is good. You did this for me?' She climbed on to my knee, squeezing me to her. 'Thank you, thank you!' She showered me with kisses. 'I hate that peeg. I am so glad.'

'No, I didn't do it for you,' I said, restraining her. 'He got on my nerves, thassall. It was a matter of survival. At least I got some peace afterwards. You don't know what it's like stuck in there with men like that. Pigs got better manners.'

'My poor darling, I can imagine.'

'Well, let's keep this between you and me. It's our secret. I don't fancy a hempen necktie. I broke the law and they could still charge me with it. I was the main suspect. Him and his gang had been amusing themselves beating me up. I had to. The screws tossed me in solitary. Six weeks in the black hole. Some guys go crazy thrown in there. But, I didn't break. They knew it was me but they couldn't prove it.'

'Poor baby. I guess you needed to speak of this. But I will never tell anyone. You did it for me, I know you did. Why don't you go to confession? The priest will keep your secret, too. God will forgive you.'

'That's big of Him,' I muttered.

'Sean, less go lie down. Maybe now you can — '

Well, we could lie down, and she would terribly arouse me, but when it came to — I knew it would be no good.

★ ★ ★

And so it proved. I was lying there staring at the ceiling when Mercedes said, 'Sean, a girl told me she see you go in that bar on Gay Street. You no *homosexuale*, are you?'

I gave a gasp of laughter. 'No, I ain't. Least, I hope not. This is something to do with my mind.'

'Then why you go there?' For the

first time I saw a touch of contempt on Mercedes' sweet face. She flickered her fingers at me. 'What matter with you? It not easy for me, you know.'

'I just go there to use their writing materials, thassall.'

'I'm sorry, Sean,' she cried, wistfully. 'I jus' wan' to make love with you, to be happy.'

'Looks like that ain't to be.'

I heard Chaco call from out in the yard, 'Riders comin'.' I only had time to roll out of bed, pull on my blue jeans and grab my carbine for I could already hear the jingle of harness, the thud of cantering hooves. Outside, I saw Chaco up on the roof of the bunkhouse. He pointed at a body of about six men approaching. Estevan was at their head, accompanied by a rider I took at first to be a youth, dressed cowboy-style in Stetson, bandanna, tight pants and boots. But, as they jogged near, I saw the telltale movement beneath the blue shirt. The bounce of what appeared to be very well-formed breasts. Here was another teenager who in five years had rounded out and become a very pretty girl. Lily Buchanan.

'Don't crowd me,' I shouted, as they jostled in close a few feet away. 'This gun might go off.'

'So might our'n,' Spike Stephens, on his mustang, snarled.

'And mine,' Chaco called, showing himself from the roof of the bunkhouse, his old bolt-action Enfield covering them.

'That broken nose ain't improved your looks or your temper much,' I grinned at Spike. 'But, then, they weren't much to begin with.'

'You — !' His hand slapped the butt of his revolver.

Estevan spoke sharply, 'Hold it!'

Steve called out from the loft of the stable behind them. 'You need any help, boss?' The riders turned, uncomfortably, and saw that he, too, had a rifle trained on them. If it came to a shooting match they might get the three of us, but we would account for several of them. And I was sure Estevan would not want Lily in the firing line.

The blonde youngster had a long-barrelled Dragoon in the holster on her hip, and a nickel-plated snub-nose Hopkins and Allen .32 stuck in her belt. So she was still acting and talking tough?

'This the one been causing Daddy all the trouble? What you waiting for, Estevan? Kill him.'

'Shut up, Lily. Your daddy don't want him dead, just yet.'

'So, what do you varmints want?' I asked.

'You wouldn't take a thousand five years ago,' Estevan said. 'Mr Buchanan has upped it to five thousand dollars.'

'What for?' Mercedes had slipped out to stand beside me. 'He don' need your money.' She was tying the sash of her skirt, tossing back her hair, proudly. 'We got our own money.'

'Yeah, I heard he was pimpin' for you,' Spike growled, as the other men laughed. 'His Mex whore.'

'He ain't pimping. We're partners. Any cash I put in his business I get back in triplicate,' she blurted out.

Spike scoffed. 'He ain't gonna have any business.'

Estevan's swarthy jaws spread into a smile. 'You nearly give Mistuh Buchanan apoplexy when he read that article today in *The Citizen*. He don't like the publicity.'

'Tough!'

'Five thousand dollars to forget your freight-train business, and to stop causin' trouble with the Mex farmers. You can come work for him at top wages. Or you can get out of the territory.'

'And if I don't?'

Estevan's hooded eyes were as fierce as a hawk's as he whispered, 'I will have to kill you.'

'If you don't,' Spike muttered, 'I will.'

'You can tell Buchanan that I want to see him crawl up to this house on his hands and knees and beg forgiveness for what he done to me. Then I might consider it.'

'He won't,' Lily said. 'This is a waste of time. Kill him now.'

'Honey.' Estevan leaned across and touched her hand, familiarly. 'Your father don't want him dead. It ain't a good time.'

She drew her hand away contemptuously. 'What's the matter? You scared of him?'

Estevan's eyes narrowed. 'Shut your mouth, Lily.'

'Bloodthirsty li'l critter, ain't she?' I smiled up at the girl. Strands of her corn-coloured hair hung from beneath her Stetson across her full girlish cheeks, and she stuck her lower lip out petulantly. Her eyes, an odd mixture, met mine. Suddenly her dark pupils widened. I was standing there barefoot in just my faded jeans, bare-chested, and I knew she was assessing my body, muscled and sunbrowned from five years rockbreaking. I had seen that look in a girl's eyes before, and something inside me stirred.

'Maybe she'd like to try me, herself?'

Mercedes had seen that look, too, and caught hold of my arm, possessively. 'Tell her to go to hell, Sean.'

Lily gave a little smile. 'What's the whore worried about?'

'Reckon you could kill me, do you. Estevan? Why don't you put those fancy pistols aside and try it with your fists?'

'Yes, go on, Estevan,' Lily jeered. 'Show him what a man you are. Beat him to pulp. He can't insult us like this.'

'Shut up,' Estevan said, rattled. 'Mistuh Buchanan might up it to six thousand. His final offer.'

'No thanks.' Maybe it was foolish bravado in front of the girl, but I grabbed hold of Estevan's left boot, twisting its silver tip into the stallion's side, levering him out of the saddle and flinging him unexpectedly to the ground. Before he could recover I dived beneath the horse's belly and pinioned him to the dust with my knees. The men whirled their mustangs away as I retrieved his silver-engraved revolvers and threw them into a corner.

'OK, *muchacho*,' I said, letting him get up. 'How about it?'

He roared like an angry bull and lunged a right and a left at me. I blocked them, and hammered my own right fist into his heart, following up fast with a flurry of blows that sent him reeling backwards against the bunkhouse wall. He recovered himself, spread his hands and whispered, 'OK, boys, keep out of this.'

He hurled himself on me, getting me in a bearhug, and I saw stars as he nutted me with his hard forehead, and yowled as he bit into my ear. I brought my knee up sharpish, and he gasped as I broke his hold.

'OK, you wanna play dirty, so can I,' I said.

My two hands clasped I hacked them across his swarthy jaw for double impact and he collapsed to one knee. I got him in a headlock and tried throttling the life out of him. I heard a crack in his throat. I could have broken his neck if I had wanted to. But I eased the pressure.

'You had enough?'

For answer he hurled me over his shoulder and sent me rolling towards the stable. I tripped over an iron chicken trough and fell headlong. Estevan snatched it up and tried to brain me. I ducked and heard it whistle past my head. I scratched up dust in a cloud into his eyes to blind him, and kicked the feeding trough from his hands. My sexual frustration, my longing for revenge, boiled up in me and I coiled my fists tight and smashed them again and again into his chest and head. We were both out of breath, slugging hard, missing more often than not, a couple of piledrivers from Estevan stopping me, dazed, in my tracks. We couldn't keep this up. One of us had to go down.

And Estevan, finally, slumped to one knee, then to both, flailing futilely, collapsing like a poleaxed bull, his bloody face in the dust. I turned from him, concerned at what the others might do.

'Sean!' Mercedes screamed. 'Watch out!'

Instinctively, I ducked, and a thin, razor-sharp knife near parted my hair, thunking with a quiver into the bunkhouse door. Estevan still had his throwing arm raised.

'That weren't fair.' I went across and kicked him back into the dust. 'You know Mister Buchanan don't want me killed just yet.'

I eased my aching knuckles, and wiped blood from my own mouth, as two of his men jumped down and helped Estevan back up. He waggled his jaw and tried to swallow his humiliation with a grin.

'You sure pack a punch.' He snapped his hands up, waving his men away, and climbed on to his stallion. His eyes were dark and sullen as he pondered me. 'There won't be any fisticuffs next time.'

I picked up his revolvers and handed them back. 'We'll see.'

'Clear out and don't come back,' Chaco yelled, as the men, and the girl, turned and rode away.

11

Chaco and Steve worked with a will and made a good job of cleaning out the well, the *casa* and their bunkhouse. I knew they had both been warned by Estevan that it would not be wise to work for me, but they were proving loyal. I set them to knocking in poles for a mule corral. Maybe soon we might even sow a field with beans. Meantime, I rode into Tucson to pick up some furniture and lumber, and take a look at the article Wesson had written about me. No wonder it stuck in Buchanan's craw. It made me sound like a knight in shining armour ready to take on the big bad boys and clean up Arizona single-handed if the law wasn't ready to. Wesson certainly had the gift of the gab. But I wasn't sure I needed a halo just yet. It made me sound kinda absurd, like some crazy Don Quixote.

The quartermaster sergeant beckoned me over, his eyes widening when he saw my puffed-up lips, the blue bruise on my cheek, the bite out of my ear a quarter-inch deep which I had dosed with *tecole*, the grease used on cows when they had their ears notched. 'What happened to you?'

'You could say I've been branded. But, he got as bad. What's the problem?'

'That consignment I gave you; I've had the top brass on to me bawling me out. The colonel says I had no right employing you, that Buchanan's got the contract. I was hoping to give you more work, save the army money, but it's no dice.'

'So Buchanan's got friends all the way up, has he?' I mumbled through my fat lips. 'Can't you go over this colonel's head? Go to the general. Explain the situation. I can give you good service.'

'I could try,' the sergeant said, doubtfully. 'I'll be in touch.'

Ned Parsons also wanted a word. 'What you trying to do, Sean, undermine my authority? This town was ticking over nicely until you come back. Why you trying to stir up trouble? You trying to lose me my job?'

'No. Wesson was only stating what I told him. That I was framed. That this territory is run by a corrupt bunch of crooks right up to the governor's mansion and beyond. And I, for one, don't intend to take it lying down.'

I left him to chew on that. He didn't like it, I knew. It crossed my mind that perhaps he, too, was on Buchanan's payroll, but I dismissed the thought as unfair. I couldn't really blame him for getting mad.

Sam and I loaded up my purchases on the wagons and headed back to the farm. There I had another visitor. Pablo Velasquez. He said they had started picking and he would have at least two wagonloads of produce ready by the morrow. He wanted me to take it up to Florence where he figured he'd get the best price. I promised to be there first thing.

★ ★ ★

'Get these wagons rolling,' I yelled as, the next morning, we set out, and I cracked the whip lavishly over the backs of my team of mules as they took the strain and settled into a trot. 'Hee-yup thar,' I hooted in true muleskinner fashion, tossing in a few blood-curdling oaths. 'Haw, Esmeralda. Haw!'

Outside Tucson, the stagecoach to Florence came hurtling past us at a headlong gallop kicking up a cloud of dust. They could afford to go at that clip. They would get a change of horses every fifteen or twenty miles at the stage stations.

We took it more steadily with our cargo, slowing for the first gradients when the trail began to wind into the foothills of the Santa Catalinas. I had shoved Sam into the back wagon to sleep off his hangover and brought

142

Chaco and Steve along for protection. Pablo, on his mule, was riding with us to get the best price for his cargo. He also made himself useful greasing the axles of the wagon-wheels — how Mex's got the name 'greaser'.

We were nearing Point Mountain when a shot barked out, reverberating through the canyon. Daisy, the nigh leader, screamed and reared and fell across Esmeralda. I hung on tight for seconds of shock as the mules plunged in panic, tangling themselves in the traces. The wagon slid sideways and, for moments, appalled, I thought we were going over the precipice. But Sam had had the sense to clamp the brake and we skidded to a halt.

Another shot whanged and whined above the racket of the frantic mules and nearly took off my hat. I grabbed my Winchester, jumped down, and ran at a crouch towards the dead mule. My first thought was that it was the Apache. My next thought was to save Esmeralda, if possible. The team was kicking and bucking and the lead mule, on her side, was lashing out with iron-shod hooves. I used my knife to slash her free, and managed to unhook the traces. Esmeralda righted herself, and the mules, in a snarl of chain and harness, lunged and stumbled, and I moved the team to the protection of a cliff wall.

That was the team safe. Our next job was to defend ourselves. I dived down behind the dead mule and peered over as bullets splatted into her. I glimpsed a man in a Stetson behind a rock among the scree of ocotillo. These weren't Apache. Judging from the shooting the bushwhackers numbered six at the most.

To take a rest in the shade, Steve and Chaco had been riding on the tongue of the trail wagon, and had quickly jumped down and taken cover when the shooting began. Maybe these *hombres* didn't know they were there? Maybe they thought it was just me and Pablo they were dealing with?

'Keep hid,' I yelled back, urgently. 'I'm gonna play doggo. Maybe they'll show themselves.'

I kneeled and loosed off my Colt Lightning at the rifleman in the rocks. He was out of range, I knew, but it drew their fire. Lead whistled nerve-shatteringly close to me. I jerked up my hands, dropped my revolver, and slumped down.

Simultaneously, there was a scream and I looked back and saw Pablo hit the ground. He had run forward out of cover. He half rose to his knees, trying to hold together with his hands the torn hole in his fat chest. Blood was pumping out. He collapsed and died trying to make the sign of the cross, a prayer on his lips.

Poor Pablo. He was certainly not play-acting. But what would the men in the rocks think about me? There was an eerie silence as I lay there and the others kept still. I listened to the indignant snorting and shuffling of the mules. Another volley of shots racketed out. But we made no reply.

It seemed like a long time before I heard the crunch of boots on the trail, and the slither as another man ploughed down through the shale on the mountainside. 'We got 'em both,' one said. Other voices joined in. 'It was a piece of cake.'

'Not both, mister,' I shouted, and raised myself to face the six gunslingers, who were strung out across the trail. I fired my Winchester carbine into the chest of the leading man, and savoured his surprised expression as he hurtled back. Behind me the guns of Chaco and Steve barked out as they showed themselves, and the six *viciosos* went down like ninepins, hardly firing a shot. My main danger was old Sam, who peppered them with both barrels of his shotgun!

'What you trying to do?' I shouted, angrily. 'Make a colander of me?'

As wreaths of black powder drifted pungently on the still air we went forward to examine the dead men, poking at them with our boots. 'They're Buchanan's men,' Steve said. 'My old *amigos*.'

'Adios, compadres,' I shouted, as we slung them off the cliff edge. 'You got an appointment with the buzzards.'

We buried Pablo Velasquez under a pile of rocks and rigged up a rough cross. He wouldn't get to market this time. We fixed up the mules and, one short, went on our way. Our only other damage was a leaking water barrel from a bullethole. I got a good price for the produce in Florence, which was busting at the seams, people flocking in to work at the new mills and breweries and commercial establishments. In spite of Apaches, Arizona was being opened up. We found a sleepy saloon in the old adobe town with its tree-lined *acequias*, ate Mex food, while Sam supped his 'medicine'. Drunk or sober, he was ready to ride the next day and we made it back in fast time with the empty wagons. I reported what had happened to Ned Parsons, and took

Pablo's cash and my sad news to his homestead. At least, he had two sons to carry on.

'Who did this?' his widow asked, her face a mask.

'Buchanan.'

'You keel him for me?'

'Waal, that's easier said than done. I might try.'

'You keel heem for me, *señor*. Please.'

I felt bad about her man. I met her eyes and nodded. In a way, his death was my fault. I owed her.

12

So, I was relaxing on my front porch, with its stone wall surround, playing, or trying to, some bamboo pan pipes I had picked up. The Hispanics, backed by drum and guitar, could make a good sound, and, for an Anglo, I wasn't doing so bad. From his nest in the rocks below the *casa*, Reggie the rattlesnake must have had his siesta disturbed, because he came sliding out of his hole to investigate. Generally he stayed in his corner, but today he slithered nearer. The fluting of the pipes seemed to fascinate him. His beady eyes were fixed on me and, at first, I thought he was going to strike. But, no, he raised his forepart, his forked tongue flickering out, and began to sway as if in a trance. I gently blew the pipes and swayed with him, entranced, too. Was this possible — an

149

Arizona snake charmer?

The spell was snapped by a shout, the sounds of a horse rider real close. I had given the boys time off to go into Tucson and get steamed, and had been so engrossed with Reggie I had forgotten the rest of the world. I sprang to my feet and saw across the wall, Lily dismounting. She appeared to be alone. 'Hi!' she called, and came towards me, dressed in a white jersey cloth, gold embroidered outfit of top and pants that clung to her nubile curves. Reggie started rattling furiously as she climbed the streps.

'Watch out for the rattler,' I said.

What the hell, I wondered, is she doing here?

Once again she had caught me bare-chested, in just my jeans. I reached out an arm to guide her. 'OK, pass the other side of me. He won't hurt you.' She brushed past close to me and she had a perfumed, womanly scent that brought a rush of blood to my body.

'So,' she said, seating herself in

an old rattan chair and giving an impish smile at the pan pipes in my hand. 'Rattlesnake-tamer, too? A man of many parts.'

'That's right.' I was having difficulty hiding mine. There was something about this girl that shot through me like a bolt of electricity. With her, I knew, I would have no difficulty. 'What brings you to my abode?'

'Guess.' She gave a girlish grin, showing her white rodent teeth between plum lips. 'Got anythin' to drink?'

'Lemonade?'

'Somethin' harder?'

'You *have* grown up. Cactus juice?'

'That'll do.'

'I've abandoned wrasslin' with the whiskey on account it was gettin' the better of me. But, I guess a coupla shots of mescal never did no harm.'

'Apart from make a man forget what he's s'posed to be doin'.'

'Yeah, well, I guess I won't forget that with you here.'

I went back into the kitchen and

found the *olla* of homebrew hanging in the shade to keep it cool. In spite of its nasty spikes the mesquite plant could be mighty useful. While I was at it I took some limes, and some goat's cheese from the muslin wrapping. I placed it on a plate before her. 'All I got is hard tack biscuits. Wasn't expectin' company.'

'You're a funny guy, aincha?'

'What do you mean?'

'Well, you act tough.' She crunched on a cracker and cheese, her mouth full. 'But you're also quite gentle.'

'What's funny about that? You act according to the occasion.' I poured her a shot, and she reached forward, real quick, and tossed it down. I cut a lime and proffered a segment. She gripped my wrist and held it while she bit in, her pink, damp tongue touching my fingers. 'And this, I gotta admit, is an occasion. The daughter of Buchanan presenting herself.'

'I hate him.'

'You what?'

'I hate him. He smothers me. I can't do anything without him trying to stop me. He sent a bodyguard after me but I gave him the slip.'

'You don't say?' I stood and looked around, but there was just sagebrush, mesquite and scrubby cactus stretching away beyond the farm. I savoured a glass of the mescal and it stirred its evil fire through me. I knew I wouldn't stop until the *olla* was dry. 'We seem to be alone.'

'That's right, big shot. I'm not exactly stupid, am I?'

'Are you asking or stating?' I took another swig and considered her. 'You certainly ain't lost your girlish charm.'

Her bright eyes fixed on me beneath the brim of her Stetson. 'Don't try to be funny with me, Flynn. I don't need patronizing. I have enough of that from my daddy. You're an old man, aincha?'

'Twenty-nine must seem pretty old to a gal like you.'

'You ain't *so* old. I liked the way you

beat up Estevan. You really made him look small.'

'He asked for it. I wasn't doing it for your pleasure.' But, I wondered to myself, was that true? Hadn't I been trying to impress her? 'You seem to have a knack of making a man feel cheap.'

Lily grinned, scoffingly again, swept off her big hat, and scraped at her blonde thatch, shaking it out. She filled her glass from the *olla* and stuffed her cheeks with more cheese and biscuits. 'You want to know what my relationship with Estevan is? He's a creep. You give him a yard and he wants a mile. He keeps grabbing me and watching me. He's worse than my pa.'

'Which means, I take it, that you and he — '

She shrugged, her cheeks dimpling, her eyes sparkling in the sunlight as she leaned towards me. 'That's for you to guess.'

Although I have tried to be factual

in relating this account of happenings in Arizona, I must admit that my mind is a little hazy about what happened next. She was leaning forwards, her legs crossed, and I was somewhat fixated by her half-unbuttoned top, the tremble of her breasts, the shadow of her cleavage. 'Christ!' I murmured, as she pouted her moist lips, and licked them with her tongue tip. 'I don't believe it.'

'Don't believe what?' she asked, with mock innocence. 'I ain't told you nuthin' yet.'

I swallowed my desire for this post-pubescent, over-endowed, sibilant and petite siren and asked, 'Like what?'

'Like I want you to kidnap me?'

'Kidnap you?' I must have sounded like Little Sir Echo.

'Yes, kidnap me. For a ransom.'

'A ransom?'

'Yes, a ransom, dim brain,' she said, irritably. 'Do you have to keep repeating me? You're supposed to be a hard man, aren't you?'

'I've done my time.'

'Yes, and I've done mine, stuck away on that lousy ranch in the hills. I want to live, go places; New York, Europe, New Orleans, every place. Instead he keeps me confined there. It's him who's kidnapped me. I've got to get away. And I need money. He won't give me any. Oh, he'll buy me a new horse or gun or dress, whatever I want. But he won't allow me any cash.'

'Can't say I can imagine you in a dress.'

'Shut up, will you? I dress the way I please. You're as bad as him. He wants me to go to the governor's ball in all those frills and fal-de-lals, mix with those tittering bitches. I don't want that life. I'm due my inheritance, but he says I can't have anything until I'm twenty-one. I can't wait that long. I'll die.'

'So, what do you want with me?'

'Kidnap me. Hide me some place for a few days. Get my father to pay a big ransom. Say forty thousand dollars. He's got it. He's got a million tucked away. Twenty for you, twenty for me. When he's paid it you send me back.'

'What happens then?'

'A few weeks later we'll skip. Head for Californya. Or south over the border.'

I gave a whistle of wonderment. 'You've sure got it worked out. What makes you think I'd want to skip with you?'

She grinned, and reached out fingers to stroke the inside of my thigh. 'Because you want me more than you want that Mex whore.'

'You're crazy. You better forget this hare-brained scheme. Kidnapping's a hanging offence.'

'You ain't gonna kill me. We're just playing a joke on my daddy if anybody finds out. But there's no reason; why should they? All I say is some nasty Mexican *bandidos* held me.'

'Nothing's as easy as that. I admit I'd like to sting your daddy. But those sort of things have a way of going wrong.'

'This can't fail. We rehearse it 'til

we're word perfect.'

'This is a trick, isn't it? Soon as it's done you denounce me to the marshal.'

'Look, there's no trick. I don't give a damn about my father's feud with you. He's acted real mean. He deserves to get taken. I like you, dumb cluck,' she said, giving a little twisted smile. 'In fact, I admire you. We could make a good team.'

'A good team,' I murmured, as she leaned forward and kissed me, her lips open and inviting, her tongue flickering like a rattler's. Just as dangerous. But I no longer cared, my mouth was dry, and I wanted her. 'Perhaps we would, too.'

'You see,' she whispered, as she slipped down between my knees and ripped the studs of my flies open. 'You're weakening.'

Perhaps I was. But I was also hard and coiled taut as a spring. I needed to unwind. My heart was beating fast, and that wasn't the only thing. When she had pleasured me on the porch almost to the ultimate, I picked her up, took her inside and threw her on the iron bed. I tore her clothes off and all the time this wild, wanton bobcat was clawing and whimpering as we made the springs bounce. When I came to we were lying on the bed, glued as tight as two people could be glued, sweat streaming from me.

'Whoo!' Lily's sage-mixture eyes looked up into mine, defiantly. 'You sure don't give a gal much time to breathe, do you, cowboy?'

I sank into her with a deep sense of bliss and relief. 'It's been a long time.'

As I lay there on the sprawled Lily I thought, maybe this is the ultimate lowdown revenge on Buchanan? To have his daughter *and* his money? I knew this was danger, this was fire, but I was tempted. It's certainly true what they say about revenge — it was real sweet.

13

Joe Wesson wrote another scorching article in *The Citizen* reporting the attack on my wagons and repeating my allegation that Buchanan's men had been the attackers. He included a denial from the big man that he knew anything about it. It was good news. That Buchanan should have spoken out meant he was going on the defensive.

Wesson also gave an account of my claim that high-ups in the army command were interfering with free trade by putting a block on using my freight. Under the headline *Teamster War Hots Up* he reported that I had been robbed of the chance of delivering a load of flour and beef to the San Carlos Reservation, even though my service was cheaper and more efficient.

I happen to know a lot of those

supplies have not been properly delivered in the past by Buchanan's, he reported me as saying. *Bags of meal have contained rocks and have even been poisoned with strychnine. I pledge that if I am given this freight nobody will tamper with my stuff. The Indians will get their due entitlement on time. At least the Indian agent will. What happens after that is not down to me. Maybe the army should supervise it being handed out.*

Buchanan must have been seething. Thank the Lord for the power of the Press. Shortly afterwards the quartermaster sergeant informed me that Colonel Nuttal had reluctantly counter-manded his order and that he was giving Flynn's Freighters the shipment of grain and beef for the Apache reservation.

'I had a word with the general and explained the situation. He was in agreement with me. If you can give us better value and service there's no reason why we shouldn't use you,' he grinned. 'You've certainly stirred things up.'

It was good news. On top of giving Buchanan's top gun a bloody nose, and killing his bushwhackers, I was feeling pretty cocksure as I supervised the loading of the wagons. The knowledge that I was functioning like a man again was a weight off my mind. Lily Buchanan's body had been like dipping into an oasis after five years in the desert. I knew she was a cheap little chiseller, but I couldn't wait to get my hands on her again. And, all the time, at the back of my mind, I was going over and over her kidnap plan. My sane mind told me to forget it, that she would only bring me big trouble. Why risk everything when I was doing so well on my own? Why chance being thrown back into Yuma prison for life?

'Ain't you coming with us?' Steve asked, when I deputed him and Chaco to accompany Sam on the journey south.

'You don't need me. You can handle this. Just keep Sam off the whiskey, thassall.'

It was with a sense of warm satisfaction that I watched the mule train pull out, old Sam cracking his snake and hollering at Esmeralda to go. That would keep them out of my way for two weeks, at least. All the time I would need. I was going to go ahead with the kidnap. I pushed rational thought behind me, all warnings that I was standing on a precipice edge. My lust for Lily, my desire to compound my revenge on Buchanan, propelled me on.

I had no intention of leaving the territory. With another $20,000 under my belt I could buy a whole fleet of freight wagons. I could put him out of business. Why, I might even start my own stage line, compete with his Tombstone run. The whole prospect excited me. I knew I couldn't trust her, that these schemes had a habit of going wrong. I must have been thinking with my *cojones*. But the plan was so simple I almost believed we could pull it off.

In The Silver Garter I was having a beer and chawin' the cud with the bartender, when Mercedes wound her wiry arm hard around my neck. 'You seem very cheerful today. Whass goin' on?'

'Aw.' I gave her a hug. 'Man cain't be gloomy all the time. Look, Mercedes, I'm going to be busy for the next few days. I don't want you coming out to the *casa*. I don't want any distractions.'

'Why?' Her sloe-dark eyes were turned on me, suspiciously. 'Sean! You got another girl, I keel her. I love you so much, I keel you, too.'

'How many men you have in a day? Don't you think that cuts me? How do you think I feel?'

'*Mi amor.*' She clutched at me. 'Pah. These men are nothing to me. It is you I want. You must not be jealous of them.'

'Typical woman's double standards.'

I grinned at the barkeep as I tried to detach her from me. 'Don't worry, honey. It's only business. Just do as I say. I'll see you on fiesta day.'

Mercedes stood hands akimbo in her flame dress outside the saloon and watched me as I rode out of town on a new black gelding I had bought. She tossed her curls, haughtily, and the look she gave me made me think, Hell hath no fury . . .

I didn't want to hurt her. In spite of her depraved profession she was a more honest, better girl than Lily Buchanan. Fate had thrown us both a lousy trick, that was all. Anyway, she didn't own me. But she was a Mex firecracker and, at the back of my mind I was uneasy. Sparks might well fly.

The gelding was a lively mount, a touch of the spurs had his hooves drumming, and I set off fast along the trail eager for that afternoon's assignation.

It was cool in the shade of the bamboo wattle canopy on my veranda. I was impatient and the minutes dragged as I waited for her. But my heart began pounding when I saw her weaving her way on her flashy white quarter-horse through the rocks from the trail to the house.

'Mind the rattler,' I said. 'Just step round him.'

'That durn thang still here?'

'He ain't hurtin' none. Come sunset he'll sidle off into the bush to hunt his supper.'

'Well, I'm here.' Lily Buchanan gave me a toothy, dimpled smile. 'We meet again.'

'Yeah.' I wanted to get hold of her neat, curved body in the tight white-and-gold fringed cowboy outfit, there and then, but I decided to straighten a few things out first. I was glad to see she had the sense to hide her horse back of the bunkhouse. My eyes swept the horizon but we were all alone apart from a passing *peon* on a burro. 'You weren't followed?'

'No. It wasn't easy, but I slipped away.'

I indicated a jug of lemonade. 'Help yourself. No liquor from now on. We've got to keep clear heads.'

'You're going to do it?'

'Yes.' I nodded. 'I guess I'm fool enough.'

'Good.' She sat down opposite and wiggled her tongue tip at me, teasingly, her eyes bright as the sky. 'When?'

'Don't it worry you riding around the countryside on your own? It's a mite risky, ain't it?'

'I go where the hell I like.' She slapped the long-barrelled revolver on her hip. 'Nobody messes with me. I'm a Buchanan.'

'What about the chance of meeting Apache? Don't that worry you?'

'No.' She was very aware of her feminine assets, but she still liked taking the male role, talking tough. 'They're bottled up in the Superstitions. I got me a rifle on the hoss. I can take what comes.'

'You could easily get snatched. Anywhere. You get my meaning?'

'Wherever you like, Marshal. I cain't wait to get my hands on my miserly daddy's cash.'

'Whatever happened to filial loyalty?'

'Huh? What's with the big words?'

'Never mind. The main thing is, if we do this, you and I got to trust each other, completely.'

'I trust you, Sean.' She showed her front teeth with a teenager's grin. 'You gotta trust me. I ain't gonna go snitching on you. What would be the point? We'd lose everything.'

'Let's get this straight: I'm not going to leave the territory. Once this is done I'll carry on with my freightin' business like nuthin' has happened. If I run away they'd come after me.'

'What about me?'

'You could leave your daddy. Come live with me. There's nothing he could

168

do. Or you can run off to Nawleans. Me, I ain't interested in them places.'

'Mmm?' She shrugged, considering this with a dreamy smile as she sipped the lemonade. 'Gal could have a lot of fun with all that cash in Nawleans. But maybe I'll stay with you. That'll really make my daddy mad. You know he'll kill you?'

'He can try. Five years ago you two seemed like chums. You wanted him to let you kill me.'

'Aw, I was just a kid. Silly ole fool. He won't give me nuthin'. Except — ach!' She shuddered, as if at the memory of something nasty. 'He thinks I'm still his little girl. You know? He says now I won't come into my inheritance until I'm twenty-*five*. I'll be an old maid by then.'

'You were pretty keen for Estevan to kill me the other day.'

'I changed my 'legiance. He's a pain. Come on, what's the grief? What you worryin' 'bout, Marshal. There's no risk.'

'There's every risk I could be put back in the slammer for life. I used to be a marshal and I know how they behave. They'll question you and go on questioning you. They'll want to know details about the men who kidnapped you. What they looked like. What they said. You've got to be word perfect. There's to be no slip-ups.'

'If I know my daddy he won't want the law brought in. He's so besotted with me he'll pay up without question.'

Again it crossed my mind that something unhealthy was going on up at Casa Grande. 'Listen, you cheeky li'l bitch.' I leaned over and grabbed her by her shirt front, pulling her face close to mine. 'This isn't a game we're playing. This is for forty thousand dollars. We've got to make it look good. We've got to convince people this is real. We don't want anybody getting suspicious. I ain't being put back in the jug just because you're too lazy or insolent to do what you're told. And, another thing, remember, if you ever blab, if you ever try to doublecross me, it will be the last thing you ever do. Savvy?'

'What you getting so het up about?' Lily tossed her head, haughtily, as I released her. 'Calm down.'

'Right. Now we understand each other. Here's what we do. There's an old copper mine up in the hills. I've often thought it would make a perfect hideout. You'll have to hide down in the dark for a week. It will be pretty eerie, but quite safe. Can you do that?'

'A week?' She looked startled. 'On my own? Why so long? I'll go crazy.'

'I spent six weeks in solitary, and I'm not crazy, am I?' I smiled at her. 'A week or maybe five days, won't hurt you. You've got to stay down the shaft, not show yourself, otherwise everything might be ruined. It will give me time to pick up the ransom.'

'I guess I can do it.'

'Good girl. I think it best we make the snatch this Saturday. You'll be coming in to the Mex fiesta won't you?'

'Yes, my daddy's taking me to the governor's ball. Wants to show me off.'

'It will be easy for you to slip away among the crowds. Make sure you wear a Spanish-looking dress and put a shawl over your head to disguise your hair. Come back here and hide in the stable loft. I'll meet you at midnight and take you up to the mine. Is that clear?'

'Why don't I just get kidnapped out in the open? Why in the town?'

'Because this way I can hang around the saloon, make sure I'm noticed, so I got some sort of alibi.'

'Marshal, you sure got a crooked mind.'

'Comes with the job. I'll have the ransom note delivered to your father at the governor's ball. I figure the first thing he'll do is start scouring the country looking for you before he realizes it's going to be in his best interest to pay up if he wants you back safe and sound. You are, after all, the apple of his eye. Though I can't think why!'

She wrinkled her nose in distaste. 'What's with the insults all of a sudden?'

'You're not so bad, I guess. Just spoiled rotten. Now, listen, this is what happens to you. You've got to remember it word perfect. Two Mexican *bandidos* hustled you away from Tucson, took you to their hideout. The first one was tall, a scar across his right cheek . . . '

I made her repeat the plan over and over. I lit cigarettes for us. 'Let's go through it once more.'

'Aw, no,' she whined. 'Give me a break.'

'Come on, once more, from the start. If Ned's called in he's going to be looking for the slightest variation in your story. You gotta get it exact.'

'These two *bandidos*, do they beat me?'

'No, they treat you reasonably well. We've got to say that because there won't be any rope burns on your wrists.'

'Where will you make him hand over the cash?'

'At those old Indian ruins up in the hills near Casa Grande. You'll be handed back once the ransom is paid.'

'I can't wait.'

'You'll have to find a hiding place in the rocks to stash your share of the cash until you're ready to vamoose.'

'Well, I ain't telling you where that'll be. You might vamoose without me.'

'Don't be silly. I could do that after the pick-up if I wanted to. You've got to trust me.'

'I guess.' She knelt down before me and ran her fingers along my thighs in their jeans, her innocent-looking eyes gazing up, desire-glazed, her mouth slightly open, her lips wet. 'I *do* trust you, Marshal.'

I picked her up in my arms and took

her into the *casa*, laid her on the rickety bed. I pulled off her boots, her tight pants. 'Don't you ever wear anything underneath?'

'No,' she smiled, dreamily.

'I assume I'm not the first?'

'No, but don't worry. There ain't many I've given my favours to.'

We took it more easily this time. And, to me, it was like sampling the various courses of a small feast. I wanted to make it last. When the final moments came she started her moaning like a small animal, sinking her front teeth into her lower lip, arching her back and striving with leaps of sensation that seemed to separate flesh from bone. 'Yes,' she cried, as her fingernails scratched down on my back. 'Yes!'

'Jeez!' she sighed, as we lay sweat-clamped together. 'I never knew it could be like that.'

The sun was going down by the time we had dragged ourselves apart. 'You better be getting back. I ought to ride part way with you, but I don't want anybody to see us together.'

'I'll be OK,' she smiled, as she dressed herself. 'I'm not afraid of the dark. I won't come here again. Not 'til Saturday.

'Sean.' She paused as she was about to get on her horse and asked, wistfully, 'You do like me, don't you? More than that Mex girl?'

'Sure,' I lied. 'Much more. But this ain't love between you and me. It's pure lust.'

14

A Mexican bugler was playing a shrill lament to mark the commencement of their religious fiesta as Frank Buchanan and his boys rode slowly into town. The discordant tone seemed somehow apt, as if announcing the scene of some new tragedy and the people flocking into church, paused to watch with solemn eyes as he passed by.

Buchanan hadn't changed much in five years. Hunched in the saddle, his hat firmly down over a face like saddle leather, his slits of eyes fixed ahead. On one side was his daughter, Lily, in her fringed cowboy outfit, on her sturdy white charger. On the other Estevan, in shiny black, on his prancing stallion. Fanned out behind them were fifteen *charros* — he was losing his gunmen fast.

If Buchanan saw me standing watching

outside The Silver Garter he gave no sign. Lily met my eye but pretended not to. They walked their horses on and drew in outside The Cosmopolitan Hotel, the classiest place in town. Buchanan, Lily, and Estevan went inside, while some of their men took up guard duty. The rest headed for a saloon.

When the dedication to some saint or other was done the Latinos streamed out of church and the fiesta began. The rest of the day would be dedicated to a bullfight by a visiting troupe from Mexico, a performance at the open-air theatre, and drinking and dancing in the streets and *cantinas* until midnight or beyond. Mercedes returned from church, an elated look in her eyes, a black mantilla over her hair. In spite of her profession, she looked as pure and spiritual as a nun.

'*Venga, hombre,*' she said, hooking her arm in mine. 'I want see the sideshows and pony races 'fore I go back to work.'

Mercedes showed a childish delight in everything as we pushed through the throng. I hoped we wouldn't bump into Lily. The last thing I needed was a catfight. In fact, we came face to face with Ned Parsons, his wife and two boys in tow. I touched my hat to Mary who said, 'I thought you were coming over to have dinner with us one night, Sean.' She pointedly ignored Mercedes.

'I been busy,' I muttered, and we went on our way, Ned looking kinda uncomfortable. 'She don't approve of you,' I told Mercedes, who was nibbling a lemon sherbert. 'Nor me, neither, come to that.'

My 'prairie nymph' looked despondent. 'Maybe one day be different.'

★ ★ ★

Everywhere were the fast strumming sounds of guitars, dulcimer, pan pipes and castanets, as people beat time with cupped hands and sandalled feet.

Groups were forming their own little parties. I pushed into the shade of the bar in Gay Street, and found a quiet corner. I called for pen, ink and paper and scrawled in Spanish in crude block letters: *Buchanan — we have your daughter, Lily. We want $40,000 in used notes. If you try to double-deal us she is gone.* I had an envelope with me addressed to him and marked *Urgent.* Inside was a lock of Lily's hair. *Next time it will be her ear. We do not want it to be her head.*

I reckoned that should scare him enough. I put the first page inside the envelope and took another page, looking around furtively to make sure nobody was watching. I dipped the pen and wrote: *You will bring the money in a pair of saddle-bags at midnight on Wednesday to the old Apache ruins at Casa Grande. You will be alone. You will see a small lamp burning. You will leave the bags beside it. The next morning your daughter will ride back to you unharmed. Be warned: if you*

*should bring men, or inform the law,
or keep watch, or try to follow, or do
anything other than what we say, you
will never see Lily alive again.*

'Hello, sweetheart. What you do?'

The transvestite's voice made me
jump as he slid into the booth next
to me. I shook the page vigorously to
dry it. 'Nothing to do with you.' I
folded the page and sealed the envelope.
'Here.' I patted him behind the head
and gave him a dollar. 'Buy yourself
a drink.' Outside it was already dark
and the parties were in full swing.

So was the governor's ball by the
time I had had myself a meal in a
cantina, and wandered along to the big
palace building. Coaches and buggies
were depositing everybody who was
considered anybody in the territory,
army officers, shopkeepers, respectable
citizens and their wives and daughters,
and members of the Tucson Ring.

'You got a ticket, *señor*?' a man on
the door asked.

'Yes. Here's my ticket.' I kneed

181

him in the groin, knocked his head back against the wall and left him in a crumpled heap wondering what had happened, as I climbed the wide staircase.

Huge chandeliers lit a long room and a military band was playing a polka, couples were dancing, others sat around, or clustered before a long buffet table helping themselves to delicacies. At one end I saw Buchanan, changed into a grey frock coat and cravat, in conversation with the governor. At an open window nearby stood Lily. She was in a dark blue Spanish dress, with purple piping, and silver pumps, fanning herself. I pushed roughly through the folks in their best clothes, staggering like I was three sheets to the wind. I grabbed a glass and spooned myself some punch.

'Get outa my way, you stuffed shirts,' I shouted. 'I used to be marshal of this town. You're all a bunch of crooks and hypocrites. I coulda proved it, but *they*' — I pointed along to Buchanan and the

Governor — 'had me railroaded.'

All eyes were on me as I swallowed the punch in one gulp. It was potent stuff. If I kept this up I wouldn't need to play drunk. From my eye corner I saw three heavies advancing on me. I turned and swung a right to the jaw, felling the first, caught hold of the second by the lapels, swung him round and hurled him at the refreshment table. He went down wrapped in a tablecloth, and covered in fruit salad and meat balls. I picked up a cut-glass bowl of trifle and rammed it on the third heavy's head, blocking his punches as he flailed.

Maybe I was overdoing it? I didn't aim to get arrested. So I raised my hands and backed away to the door. 'Sorry to disturb you folks,' I slurred. 'Guess I've had too much. *Adios*.'

I stumbled away down the staircase. The man on the door was just getting to his feet, rubbing his head. I doubted if anyone would come after me. Drunks were ten-a-penny on a night like tonight. They would just tut-tut and say, 'He's really gone to the dogs.' I hoped my little diversion would have given Lily the chance to disappear.

I hung around in the gloom of an alleyway opposite the lit-up mansion. The music had resumed and I assumed the ball was once more in full swing. A Mex kid was sitting on a stoop nearby. I whistled him over, took the envelope from my pocket, tossed him a quarter and said, 'Go give this to that man on the door. OK?' He grabbed the coin eagerly and ran across. I watched him poke the envelope at the man I had kneed. He spoke to the boy who pointed back towards me. I stepped back into the shadows.

★ ★ ★

The Silver Garter was doing holiday business. It was late and the men were lined three-deep along the bar, shouting for drinks. Estevan Zamoa was leaning against it with a couple of his men. I weaved in, doing my drunk act, pushed in nearby him and hollered to be served. Estevan gave a mocking contemptuous laugh. I grinned and saluted him. He turned his back on me and watched the floor show, Mercedes and two other girls up on a small stage kicking up their knees and swishing their skirts.

After a while, Frank Buchanan pushed his way through the batwing doors and my beer arm froze half-way to my lips. Buchanan's eyes and mouth were tense. He looked worried. He located Estevan, strode over to him and spoke to him brusquely. Estevan shook his head and snapped out some order to his men, who began to gather round him.

My blood ran cold as Buchanan suddenly met my eyes. Here was the demon who had incarcerated me.

'Buchanan,' I shouted over the heads of men who began to move back to give us room. 'Any time you're ready,

I am.' I took a lurching step to one side, my hand hovering over my gun holster, trying to look dazed.

His eyes were like stones as he regarded me. I knew he had received the letter and was wondering if I had anything to do with it. A frown of contempt dismissed the idea, dismissed me as a drunk. He carefully opened his coat to show he was unarmed.

'Guns ain't allowed at the governor's ball,' he snarled. 'Some other time, punk.'

He stomped out, followed by his men, all bar Estevan. He swaggered up to me, his silver spurs jingling, his fingers stretched out over the pearl handles of his revolvers.

'You ought to shut your mouth, Flynn. Mr Buchanan is pretty handy with a gun. You try to take on him you take on me as well.'

'I'm interested in the man at the top, not his hired hand,' I said, turning back to my drink. 'Get lost.'

'You see?' Estevan called. 'Underneath

186

he's yellow.' He turned on his heel and hurried after the others.

The joint had gone quiet and even the roulette wheel had ceased spinning. They all looked at me as if I was something the cat had brought in. Good. I wanted them to notice me. It was unlikely I would be a kidnapper if I was in here challenging the man who had tried to ruin my life to a duel.

'Yeah! What's happened to the music? Why ain't them gals dancin'?' I picked up my glass and hurled it at the mirror and bottles behind the bar.

Mercedes ran up and cried, 'Whass matter with you?' She guided me out of the door like a mother with a child who hadn't yet learned to walk straight. 'You better go home, sleep it off.'

15

The *casa* was in darkness when I got back. I gave a whistle and Lily poked her head from the stable loft. 'My father and his men have been here,' she hissed. 'They took a quick look around and galloped off back up towards Casa Grande.'

'Good. You ready to go?'

Lily had left her white mare in Tucson and had the sense to come out here on a stolen *burro*. She climbed on it and followed me as we headed through the moonlit chasms up into the hills. 'How much further?' she moaned, after two hours' riding.

'Here we are.' The sterile terraces of the former copper mine stretched out before us. 'See them soo-aros?' I pointed to a small forest of cactii on the hillside. 'It's behind them. Nobody would ever notice it.'

We climbed up through their silhouetted sentinels on foot, leaving the broncs below. I didn't want to leave a heavy trail. There was only the slit of a gap, hidden behind rocks. I lit a carbide lamp and led the way in. The tunnel gradually got smaller and we had to stoop down. There was a cold, musty smell. We came to a ledge which opened on to a gaping shaft. 'Whatever you do, don't touch these rotten timbers,' I said, echoingly, 'or you could cause a fall.'

She watched me tying a coil of rope to a rock and said, 'You expect me to go down there?' Her voice had a nervous shrillness in the silence. 'Are you mad?'

'You want to call it off after we've got so far? You scared?'

She stared coldly at me, and jutted her chin. 'No.'

'Come on,' I urged, tossing the rope-end down. 'Follow me.' I swung out and lowered myself down the near vertical descent for about forty feet until

I touched firm ground. I had tucked the lamp into my belt but was otherwise surrounded by pitch blackness. 'Where are you?' I shouted up. A shower of pebbles on my head told me she was coming.

'Where now?' she asked, as she dropped into my circle of light.

'Good girl.' I squeezed her hand and, keeping hold of it, led her along another tunnel to a cavern. 'Welcome to your lil retreat. All you got to watch out for is not to step on any of these stubs of dynamite they left around. And, for God's sake, don't go exploring down any of these other tunnels or you might never find your way back.'

I had visited the hide-out on previous days and brought blankets, water, a tin box of food, spare carbide lamps. 'There's enough for seven days, but you won't be here that long.'

Lily stood in her dusty Spanish dress, with its ruffles and puff sleeves, and suddenly looked like a kid about to burst into tears as she peered around the shadowy cavern. 'I can't stay here,' she wailed. 'It's horrible.'

'Look there's sweets and lemonade and cakes. You can pretend like you're having an extended midnight feast. I brought you a book by an English guy called Dickens. Improve your mind. Just sit around and talk to yourself and sleep.'

'Aren't you leaving me a gun?'

'You start blasting off a gun these timbers well might collapse. There's nothing down here to be afraid of. Just live in this area. Anything you gotta do you can go up the passage a bit. But not too far. If anybody, not my voice, should shout down to you, don't reply. But I'm pretty sure nobody knows about this place. Just have a nice rest.'

'No!' She clutched hold of me. 'I'm not staying. The deal's off. I can't stand this place. I'm going back to my daddy.'

She started back to the rope. When

I caught hold of her she screamed hysterically. I struck her a hard backhander across her cheekbones, threw her down on her makeshift bed.

'I ain't gone to all this trouble for you to back out now. I want that cash. In a few days it'll be ourn.'

She was quietly sobbing, rubbing her cheek. 'Nobody's ever hit me before.'

'Maybe they should have. Anyway, that bruise is gonna make it look real.' I kneeled down and stroked her face, soothing her. 'Pull yourself together. You're a big girl now.'

She nodded, tearfully. 'OK. I guess.'

'Here, I'll leave you my watch. That way you can count the days. Wednesday night I should be back.'

Her orbs of eyes followed me fearfully as I backed away, caught hold of the rope and began the climb back up. When I reached the ledge I coiled the rope up after me. I peered down the shaft and heard her shout. 'You're not taking the rope? Please don't!'

'We can't have you climbing up

out and spoiling everything,' I hissed, feeling real mean. 'So long, honey. Relax.'

I was relieved, myself, to be back in God's open air, hear night sounds after that eerie silence, see the moon up above. I used my jacket to brush out our footprints, returned to the gelding and packjack. As I rode away I felt kinda sorry for Lily left back down there. But she would just have to bear up.

16

Tucson was quiet and hungover on the Sunday morning. The tolling of a bell summoned to church those Latinos who had camped out on the plaza. After the service and a little desultory drinking they would start to drift back to their homes. In The Silver Garter I had a beer and paid for the damage I had done.

Ned Parsons came in looking for me. 'You durn fool, I nearly had to arrest you last night. But I already had a tankful of drunks.' He lowered his voice. 'Something's happened. Can you keep this to yourself?'

I took a draught of my beer. 'Sure.'

'I've reason to believe Lily Buchanan's been kidnapped. The governor's been on to me. He says a letter was delivered to Buchanan last night at the ball. When he opened it a lock of blonde hair fell out. Buchanan went as white as a ghost.'

'You don't say?' I tried to sound surprised. 'I had an idea something was wrong. He came in here, then he and his boys rode off in a hell of a hurry. Why you telling me this, Ned?'

'Look, I want you to know I ain't in Buchanan's pay. I admire what you're doing for them Mex farmers, Sean. In my book you're straight.'

'So?'

'I'd like you to help us take a look for her. You know these hills round here better than any other man. I only got Tom Stanton and Jesse Owens as deputies. Me and Jesse are going to circle around north up by the Circle K spread. Tom's gonna go south to Nogales. I thought you might look around that old silver mine in Snake Canyon, or up in the Tularosa Cave. Anywhere else you think she might be held prisoner.'

'Why should I help Buchanan?'

'She's only a teenager, Sean. A frightened kid. There were two bad-looking Mex *viciosos* hanging around yesterday. I told them to get out of town. If they got anything to do with this they're the sort who'd just as soon slit her throat.'

'Yeah, I saw those two guys. They might well be your men. OK, I ain't got a lot to do. I'm waitin' for my wagons to get back. I'll do what I can. If I meet up with those two shall I try to bring 'em in?'

'Don't do anything to panic them. We want Lily back in one piece. Here, look, I better give you a badge. Even low-lifes like them think twice before they shoot at a deputy marshal.'

I smiled at the irony as I pinned my badge on my shirt. 'Feels good to be back.'

'You're officially deputized. Ten dollars a day with expenses, OK?'

I grinned even more. It was chicken feed. I had a fortune coming to me. 'Seems to me if Buchanan hasn't asked for your help, Ned, our hands are somewhat tied.'

'That's why we got to keep this quiet. By the way, Sean, that fire we had. All the files weren't destroyed. I still got the one on Buchanan in my safe.'

'You have? That's good, because I've been getting a lot more information about what he's been up to, from Steve, from old Sam. Murder. Corruption. Poisoning the Apaches. How about reopening the case?'

'We'll see,' he said. 'First we got to get Lily back.'

'Aw, the li'l tramp's probably run off to see one of her Mex boyfriends. But it's a deal. I help you look, you help me.'

We shook hands and I went out and jumped on my black gelding and headed out of town. 'Well, hoss,' I muttered to him. 'Don't this beat everything? That dimwit wants me to capture myself.' I would do a little leisurely searching just to make it look good. 'Poor old Ned. He ain't got a clue.'

★ ★ ★

The next morning I watched out of the window of The Silver Garter and, sure enough, soon after the bank opened Buchanan rode in. He took his saddle-bags inside. When he came out they looked to be pretty full. I watched Ned approach and speak to him. Buchanan shouted angrily, got back on his horse and rode off. I went over to the marshal's office.

'I ain't had no luck, Ned. How about you.'

'Naw.' He made a downturned grimace. 'Buchanan told me if he had any troubles he'd deal with them his own way. He said he didn't want the law, me or anybody, poking their nose into his affairs.'

'Looks like we're hogtied.'

'Even worse. The manager of the bank has just told me Buchanan has drawn out forty thousand in cash. He stipulated used notes. Looks like he's going to pay out.'

'Well,' I said. 'That's up to him, I suppose. There's nothing we can do.'

'Except keep searching. Where the hell I wonder, will he make the drop?'

'That's anybody's guess.'

'Can you keep a watch out near the Casa Grande? When Tom gets back I'll send him up to help you. Me and Jesse will make a sweep of the ranches and farmsteads to the west. We'll have to search your place, too.'

'Of course. Help yourself to lemonade.'

* * *

The tension of waiting was getting to me. I tossed and sweated on my iron bed filled with bad dreams of slamming prison doors. At least my days were occupied. It would be worse for Lily trapped down in that shaft. On the Tuesday evening I got back from keeping watch near the Casa Grande, everything strangely quiet up there. I was lying on my cot when I heard the shuffling pitter-pat of a donkey's hooves. Mercedes!

'What the hell do you want? Haven't I told you I don't want you bothering me out here?'

'Why you treat me like this, Sean?' She tried to wind her arms around me, a concerned expression on her exquisite face, her soulful eyes half-hidden by the tumble of black curls. Her dark limbs in the flame dress enticed me. Maybe now I could — 'Darling, what's wrong?'

'My nerves are shot, thassall.' I threw her away. 'Get outa my hair. Get back to your damn saloon. Maybe I'll see you Saturday.'

'Maybe. She chewed her lip, considering me. 'Maybe not.'

When she had gone I breathed a sigh of relief. I hated treating her bad. When this was over I'd explain.

Tom Stanton contacted me. I suggested that if he kept watch on the Casa Grande ranch by day I'd take over by night. He readily agreed to this. It would give him a chance to get home and get some shut-eye. Everything was falling into my lap, but I couldn't shake off that sense of imminent doom . . .

When I rode up to take over from him on the Wednesday late afternoon I watched him head back to Tucson: a hard man, dressed like a 'puncher, a carbine in his saddle boot. Then I turned my gelding's head towards the old copper mine. It was near sundown by the time I reached there. I was worried about Lily. I needed to reassure her and myself that all was well. You never knew what that kid might do. I checked that I was alone and made my way up on foot through the saguaros, their arms raised to the blood-red sky.

'Lily!' I peered down the dark shaft. 'Lily, are you there?'

'Sean!' Suddenly there was a pool of light and her red-ravaged eyes were staring up at me. She was gibbering and sobbing like someone demented. 'Oh, thank God it is you. Get me out of here.'

'Hang on,' I shouted down. 'There's only a few more hours to go to midnight then I'll have the money.'

'No!' Her screams cut through me, echoing through the caverns. 'No! Please! I can't stand it.' She was drumming her fists on the shaft wall. 'Don't leave me.'

'Aw, jeez,' I muttered, and tossed the rope down. 'Wimmin!'

When I hauled her up she caught hold of me, hanging to my shirt with her nails, her face tearstained like a child's. 'Oh, God!' she shuddered. 'Get me out.'

Out in the afterglow of the fast disappearing sun, she calmed down a bit. But she was still shuddering as I hoisted her up to ride behind me. She locked her arms around me as if she never wanted to let me go.

Back at the *casa* I laid her on the bed and gave her a shot of tequila to cheer her up. I lay beside her and put an arm around her, and gradually she was soothed. She was barefoot, still in the blue silk Spanish dress, now torn and dusty. Her toenails and hands were scratched and bleeding as if she had tried to climb up the rock walls. 'I thought I would never get out of there,' she whispered. 'I thought you had left me for dead, you bastard.'

I kissed the hair like ripe corn and tried to reassure her. 'You gotta trust me, Lily.' I consulted my watch on its chain around her neck. 'Eight o'clock. Soon we're gonna be rich.'

'I don't care any more,' she murmured, snuggling into me. 'I just want to be safe.'

'Hey, I got an hour before I go.' Her young body had aroused me. 'Why don't we — ?'

'No,' she protested. 'Not yet. I don't feel — '

But the pent-up urge in me would brook no gainsay. Soon I had her under me and we were locked together making energetic love. 'No,' she moaned, clinging to me. 'No!'

★ ★ ★

A big silver moon hung low in the night sky was casting a ghostly glow across the *barrancas* and arroyos as I pounded along the lonesome trail out to Casa Grande on the black horse. His long legs ate up the distance. The Casa Grande ruins were off at a tangent five miles from the *rancho* so I cast off on a sheepherder's back trail I knew. Occasionally, I would rein in behind a big rock to see if anyone was following, but in that desolate landscape it was like being the last man on the planet. These mountains were little visited, mainly the haunt of a few *peon* sheepherders with their scrubby bell-tinkling flocks.

It wasn't them I was worried about. It was anyone else skulking around. I was wearing a disguise of split-tailed duster coat, high-pulled bandanna and tall Texan hat — normally I wore a flat-crowned Stetson and buckskins. I had no wish to kill anybody, but I was playing for high stakes and if anybody got in the way, well . . . too bad.

Half a mile from the ruins I hitched my horse to a juniper bush in the shelter of some rocks and climbed up on foot. I kept my Winchester carbine cocked in my hands, and looked behind every clump of cactii and creosote, up every gully, up at the crown of every one of the tall jumbled rocks in case someone tried to rope or shoot me. I froze when I saw a movement on one. But it was only a lone wolf watching me. Silhouetted against the great globe of moon he raised his head and gave a mournful howl. It was like a warning.

A shriek nearby made me start. It was only one of the night predators, a bobcat, maybe, pouncing on some unsuspecting kangaroo rat. Out here it was kill or be killed. Tonight that had to be my rule.

The mysterious Casa Grande ruins

were up high on the mountain. I had chosen this spot because most Indians, Mexicans and white men, too, regarded them as being haunted and stayed clear. As I walked into the box canyon the cave rooms cut high into the walls of red rock gave me a spooky feeling. It was as if someone was watching. And not just ghosts. Buchanan could have his men secreted all around in the caves to cut me down. But, why kill the ransom collector? He wanted his daughter back. Maybe he might try to capture me alive, torture me, force me to tell him where she was? I steeled myself and went on.

Somebody — was it Shakespeare? — said a coward dies many times. Well, I didn't consider myself a coward, but I died a few times that night. My heart was banging in my ribcage as I knelt down to light the hurricane lamp I had brought and left it in the central courtyard. And banging even more as I climbed up to one of the high cave rooms and entered its eerie darkness.

It was deathly quiet. I'm not one to believe supernatural nonsense, but that place made the hair on my scalp prickle. It was as if someone else was there. I told myself it was imagination, consoled myself that every man knows fear. It's nature's way of keeping him alert to danger. If you don't have stealth and caution in this country you don't stay alive long.

As I settled down to watch, my mind filled with thoughts of the Indians, the Anazazis, the Hohokama, the Mogollon peoples whose pit houses dot the hills along the Gila River. Their red-on-buff pottery, their shells, their baskets and figurines had more in common with the Mayans in the jungles of Mexico. I figured they built their pueblos like this high on the cliff walls to escape the Apache who had come from the north, and whose warlike cruelty deterred even the Conquistadors. Some, like Geronimo, still fought on. Freedom or death!

My mind-wanderings as I waited

were suddenly jolted back to reality. The shadowy shape of a horse and rider had entered the mouth of the canyon. He paused, looking about him. It was Buchanan. I gripped my Winchester tight and aimed at him. He saw the flicker of my hurricane lamp and nudged his mustang forward. There was the sound of shod hooves on rock, the creak of saddle leather. It was so quiet I could almost hear his breathing. He circled the lamp, looking about him, reached back and raised a pair of saddle-bags in his hand as if signalling to me, to whoever was watching. He threw them down to the ground and walked his horse back out of the canyon. I heard him go thudding away.

Just gone midnight. He was dead on time. But I was wary. What if he and his men were waiting for me to come out of the canyon? It was a chance I would have to take. I braced myself, climbed down and went over to the saddle-bags. They felt good and heavy. I undid the buckle of one, peered in. The lamplight showed wads of greenbacks. I gave a low whistle, my heart racing, not with fear, but excitement this time. I slung the bags over my shoulders and, carbine in hand, started back down the mountainside. There was a movement in the rocks. I nearly stumbled over whatever, whoever it was. Beady eyes gleamed in the moonlight. A scaly head. A Gila monster. A venomous overgrown lizard some four feet long. I scrambled away as it lunged for me and ran on down the hill without looking back. I leaped on to the black gelding and, when we reached the white trail, put spurs to him . . . the night sky was beginning to lighten as the houses of Tucson came in sight.

* * *

I put the horse in the stable and went in by the back door of the *casa*. It was dark inside, but by the light of the waning moon through the window,

I could see a girl's shape lying on the iron bed. Lily, her blonde mop. She was still wearing the Spanish dress she had on earlier. She must have fallen asleep. I lit a candle and sat beside her exhausted but jubilant ready to slide in on top of her.

'Hey, honey!' I shook her shoulder. 'Wake up! Look what I got! We're rich!' She moved back and forth, but, I suddenly realized, without any sign of life. My heart began to sink into my boots. I put my fingers to her neck. There was no pulse. Her head rolled back, her eyes stared at me, but with no light in them. Her tongue protruded obscenely, and there was a red mark from her mouth to her throat. I had seen many corpses, but hers made me want to throw up. 'Jeesis!' I whispered.

Suddenly I knew the feel of a hairy hempen rope around my neck, the trapdoor opening beneath me, and I was falling through, falling, falling . . . the rope jerked tight and my neck snapped. Wasn't that the meaning of the term 'the fall guy'? Wasn't that what I was?

My fingers were shaking as I unbuckled the saddle-bags. I took out the wads of notes. Cold sweat trickled down my temple. Boy, I needed a drink. I stood there stunned, looking at Lily's corpse. The bottle rattled against the tumbler as I poured a tequila. My hands were trembing. I was really scared now. The image of the scaffold hovered over me. It was not the way I wanted to go. The tequila fired through me and I controlled my panic. I had to think of a way out of this. I forced myself to examine Lily, swallowing in disgust. Blue bruises on her slim white neck, put there by the fingers and thumbs of a strong man. She had been strangled to death.

Suddenly horses clattered into the yard. I spun towards the front porch with thoughts of escape. But I was so stunned it was as if I was frozen to the spot. What was the good of running?

Ned Parsons pushed through the bead curtain over the door, his revolver at the ready. He glanced at me, the cash in my hands, and the body on the bed, with distaste. Tom Stanton and Jesse Owens followed him in.

'She's dead,' Tom said, after he had checked, as Jesse relieved me of my six-shooter. 'Caught him red-handed.' Tom brought the butt of his carbine up and cracked me across the jaw. Next thing I knew I was down on one knee spitting blood.

'Hold it. Put the cuffs on him,' Ned shouted. 'He'll get his just desserts.'

'I never did trust him,' Jesse growled, stuffing the wads of notes back in the saddle-bags.

'Boys,' I said, feeling my jaw. 'I know it looks bad but I didn't kill her. We were lovers.'

'Tell that to the judge.'

'Guess you're surprised to see us, Flynn,' Jesse Owens said. 'I made enquiries in the Hole-in-the-Wall. One of them weirdos told me he saw you the other night writing a note in block letters. Like a ransom note. That's what put us on to you.'

'Come on,' the marshal said. 'We'll take this cash back to its rightful owner. See what he's got to say.'

'Yeah.' Owens jabbed his revolver into me. 'I ain't so sure we'll be able to protect him.'

'Put Lily over that mule in the stable. Might as well take her with us. It's going to be a bad day for Buchanan.'

17

Dawn brought a pale pink flush to the sky as we rode back up the trail towards Casa Grande. I had my wrists cuffed in irons in front of me. Ned in front, the two deputies on either side, Lily's body on the mule on a trail rope behind. There was no way I could get away, of that I was sure. If Buchanan didn't shoot me, I would be taken back and hanged.

We were halfway there when I saw a movement off in the cactii and creosote bushes on the hillside. White-shirted figures, with red headbands, creeping down towards us. An arrow hissed, entered Ned's chest and stuck out of his back. 'Apache!' I screamed.

I jerked my gelding round and spurred him cruelly up the opposite hillside making for a fallen tree and a clump of rocks. I could hear the other two following me. We hurled ourselves behind the rocks as arrows rained about us. 'For Chrissake,' I shouted. 'Give me a gun.'

Owens glanced across at me, his face grim, and tossed me my Lightning. I cocked it with my cuffed hands. The Apache, crouched low, were dodging from rock to rock. There were about twenty of them. Ned Parsons was lying on his back on the trail. They had caught his horse and pulled free the carbine. Bullets began to whang and ricochet about us. We returned fire and I saw three of them topple in their tracks.

Another of the savages had pulled Lily from the mule. As she fell into the dust he jumped on her, carved her yellow hair from her head. He gave a whoop of triumph.

'Look what they done to Lily,' Owens sobbed, and emptied his carbine at them, the shots clattering out.

An older warrior stood, a lance in his hand. He ran up the hill towards us, his face a cruel-set mask, his sun-blackened thighs naked, bowed and powerfully muscled. I knew it was Geronimo. It was said he could run seventy miles in a day. Over this sort of terrain they didn't bother with ponies. We aimed at him but he seemed to have a charmed life. He hurled the lance and it thunked into the dead tree an inch from my head.

'Aagh!' Jess Owens hurtled back as a slug hit him between the eyes. He lay there out cold, blood trickling from the hole in his head. That was two of us gone. I wriggled along to him and took his carbine, unbuckling his gunbelt as Stanton held them off.

I tried to concentrate on reloading as bullets and arrows rattled about us. It was difficult. With my hands in irons. I had to use my teeth to help. The Apaches went into a high-pitched chant as they began a charge up the hill, fearless of our lead. I managed to lever slugs into the breech and sent a fusillade of shots their way.

216

Three more hit the dust, dead or injured. The others were having second thoughts. What, after all, did they want with us? They were looking for easier prey, caravans of Mexicans coming up from Sonora, freighters pulled by mules carrying food or guns, civilians out driving buggies, women, children and ponies to capture, take back to their lairs in the mountains.

We had a good position, plenty of ammunition. It would be a costly, lengthy operation to smoke us out. Our ammunition wouldn't last forever, but by that time help might have arrived. Our first fierce exchanges of lead and arrows dulled. The fight became a stalemate of sporadic firing.

'Get back, you heathen,' Tom shouted, and took some quick shots as he saw them dodging back down the hill.

'They've had enough.' I saw Geronimo go bounding away. He picked up a wounded Indian and hefted him over his shoulders, running off across the trail. We watched as they went creeping away through the scrub on the other side. We sent some parting bullets in farewell.

Tom shouted excitedly, 'Filthy savages!' He ran down the slope to look at the dead Apaches, pulled the knife and started hacking off their scalps. 'These are worth a hundred dollars' bounty,' he yelled.

I didn't want to do it. I hesitated a good while. Maybe his fascination with his grisly work made it easier for me, the obvious joy he was taking in it. He stood between me and freedom. His death or my life. I fired the carbine from the hip and he crumpled into the thorns. He lay, holding on to his gut, blood trickling through his fingers. 'You bastard,' he gritted out. I finished him with two more in the heart.

When I had unlocked the cuffs with his keys I caught my black gelding and glanced around the scene of carnage, the corpses of three white men, six Apaches and one white girl. I went over to Lily and almost retched at the sight of the flies buzzing about her scalped head. I pulled an arrow from the quiver of one of the dead Indians, drew it back and stabbed it hard into Lily's chest. As an afterthought I put the cuffs back on Stanton's belt.

I rode back towards Tucson at a hard lope along the winding trail, the saddle-bags of cash draped over my arm. I needed to hide this. I galloped into the yard of the *casa* and went inside to get a spade.

'Howdy,' Estevan said. 'Just the man I was hoping to see.' He was leaning against the wall behind the doorway, his silver-engraved Sidewinder trained on me. 'You can toss them saddle-bags on the bed.'

'So, it was you?'

'Me?' His lips curled back over his teeth. 'Me what?'

'You who killed her.'

'Take that revolver out nice and easy and place it on the bed. With two fingers. Don't try anything.' There was nothing I could do but obey. 'So you got it all figured out? Well, I guess, as you won't be alive much longer, I can tell you. Sure I killed her. She was a conniving little bitch.'

'You didn't have to kill her.'

'Didn't I?' His expression became fierce, his eyes steely. 'That bitch was going to run away with me. We were going to take her daddy's money and go south of the border. We had it all planned. And then you came along. Lily took me for a sucker. But I wasn't that stupid. I let you carry out her plan for me.'

'So, you knew all the time?'

'Get over against that wall near the door.' Estevan stooped down and unbuckled one of the saddle-bags, flicking through the dollars. He gave a whistle. 'Sure I knew. You done all the work for me. I been watching you.' He gave a sneer. 'You and her.'

'She sure was a beaut in bed, wasn't she? It seems a waste.'

I wanted to rile him, get him to

make a false move, but I was faced by an iron-nerved young psychopath. His eyes smouldered, angrily. 'When I came here last night I told her I was going to kill you, take the money. I offered to let her come with me. She laughed in my face. She treated me like dirt. Yes, I killed her. She deserved everything she got.'

'If you killed her in jealous passion you might get off with life.'

'Cut the crap.' He picked up the saddle-bags and stepped towards the front porch. 'We're going for a walk. Up towards the rocks. Somewhere where they won't find you for a bit.' He grinned at me. 'What I wasn't prepared for was Ned Parsons turning up. I watched them take you off and thought I'd lost this little lot. What happened?'

'Fate intervened.' I swung the window shutter out against him as he stepped past. It slammed against his gunhand. My left fist smashed into his jaw. The Sidewinder exploded as he stumbled back through the door. The bullet scorched past my ear. I kicked out my boot from the hip, caught him on the thigh. He tumbled back out across the stone veranda. But although on the ground, he still had the revolver in his grip and it was trained on my heart. This time he didn't intend to miss. I expected to be blown into oblivion. There was a flash of gold diamond pattern, raised fangs and a stab as fast as lightning. Estevan screamed as he was bitten in the neck.

Reggie had his head up, his tongue flickering, his rattle rattling. He slowly backed off as I appeared, and slithered back to his hole.

'Do something.' Estevan had dropped the revolver in his alarm and I kicked it away. 'Get this poison out of me.'

'Looks like the jugular. If so you ain't got long.'

'Help me.'

'Why should I? What did you do for Lily? What did you do for me? You helped Buchanan frame me, didn't you?'

'Yeah, I'll tell you everything. Just bite this poison outa me. Get the doc. Buchanan made me kill that stage driver, Hitchens. Then he got me to plant that bullion in your well. Thassall. *Do* something.'

'You've been a bad boy, Estevan. I'm afraid I've got to let you die.'

I tipped the $40,000 into a tin box, took the spade and carried it out to the edge of the field, dug a hole beneath a rock and covered it. When I got back Estevan was unconscious. I hefted him up, put him over my horse and took him along to the disused well at the back of the property. I dropped him in, tossed the empty saddle-bags on top of him.

I galloped the gelding into Tucson screaming 'Apache!' I tumbled from my horse outside The Silver Garter as a crowd came running. 'They got Ned Parsons and Lily Buchanan with their first arrows. We took cover. It was Geronimo. They shot Jesse in the head. Tom suddenly went crazy and rushed out. They killed him, too. Then faded away into the brush.'

A posse was formed to go out to recover the bodies and maybe take scalps. 'Halfway to Casa Grande. I can't go back. My hoss is done in. Me, too.' I was, in fact, wobbling on my legs. Someone caught me as I collapsed. It had been a long night.

18

Frank Buchanan looked grey and drawn beneath his tan as he followed the hearse and its prancing black horses out to Tucson cemetery. From the cemetery gates I watched as they lowered Lily's coffin into the grave. The preacher chanted his words, his black robe flapping in the wind, as Buchanan kneeled and watched the earth shovelled in. Poor girl, I thought. She didn't have a chance. I rode back and waited outside The Silver Garter, saddened by it all.

There had been an inquest into the deaths of Lily and the three lawmen. I repeated what I had said before. I had been working as a deputy marshal with them, searching for Lily Buchanan, who had been kidnapped. We had found her in an old copper mine. She told us her kidnapper, Estevan

Zamoa, had escaped with the ransom money. We never caught him. We had been taking Lily back to Casa Grande when we were attacked by Apache. Ned Parsons and Lily had been the first to die, arrows in their hearts . . .

The coroner remarked that apart from the arrow wound, Lily appeared to have been strangled. 'It's possible the Apache finished her off like that,' he said. 'If the law had been called in earlier, this young woman might still be alive today.'

The mayor of the city had asked me if I would consider staying on as deputy marshal temporarily, as nobody else wanted the job. I agreed and set about posting notices for the arrest of Estevan. Meanwhile, I got the boys to help fill in with rocks that old well on the farm.

Today, the day of the funeral, Buchanan rode back into town and stepped down outside The Garter. He glanced at me as he climbed the steps, his face stony. I caught hold of his arm and slapped the summons into his palm as he passed. I almost felt sorry for this lonely man as I said, 'You're to face a jury on curruption and murder charges. This time I'm going to make sure it's *you* who gets five years.'

As I walked back across the wide dusty street to my office I heard him shout out, 'Flynn. I've had about all I can take from you.' I turned and saw him standing on the steps, pulling a Smith & Wesson .44 from his holster. He stared at me with loathing as he aimed and fired. I stepped aside and went for my Lightning. I saw the flash of his shot as I brought it out, hit the hammer, and squeezed out a slug. His bullet tore through the sleeve of my shirt. Buchanan's face retched with pain as he clutched his abdomen and he toppled down the steps. As he expired in a pool of his own blood I could hardly believe he was dead after all this time.

'Sean, watch out!' Mercedes stepped out from the saloon, a rifle in her hands. I ducked to my knees as an explosion clapped out from behind me and a bullet snarled across my shoulder and into the dust. Mercedes aimed and fired. I looked back up and saw Spike Stephens on the roof of the undertaker's. He cried out, spun around, dropped his carbine, and landed with a thud in the dust.

Mercedes ran to me and I caught her in my arm. 'Thanks,' I said, looking around, my revolver at the ready. 'I reckon it's all over now.'

'Or, maybe' — she smiled up at me — 'it just begun. For us.'

THE END

THE CROOKED SHERIFF
John Dyson

Black Pete Bowen quit Texas with a burning hatred of men who try to take the law into their own hands. But he discovers that things aren't much different in the silver mountains of Arizona.

THEY'LL HANG BILLY FOR SURE:
Larry & Stretch
Marshall Grover

Billy Reese, the West's most notorious desperado, was to stand trial. From all compass points came the curious and the greedy, the riff-raff of the frontier. Suddenly, a crazed killer was on the loose — but the Texas Trouble-Shooters were there, girding their loins for action.

RIDERS OF RIFLE RANGE
Wade Hamilton

Veterinarian Jeff Jones did not like open warfare — but it was there on Scrub Pine grass. When he diagnosed a sick bull on the Endicott ranch as having the contagious blackleg disease, he got involved in the warfare — whether he liked it or not!

BEAR PAW
Nevada Carter

Austin Dailey traded two cows to a pair of Indians for a bay horse, which subsequently disappeared. Tracks led to a secret hideout of fugitive Indians — and cattle thieves. Indians and stockmen co-operated against the rustlers. But it was Pale Woman who acted as interpreter between her people and the rangemen.

THE WEST WITCH
Lance Howard

Detective Quinton Hilcrest journeys west, seeking the Black Hood Bandits' lost fortune. Within hours of arriving in Hags Bend, he is fighting for his life, ensnared with a beautiful outcast the town claims is a witch! Can he save the young woman from the angry mob?

GUNS OF THE PONY EXPRESS
T. M. Dolan

Rich Zennor joined the Pony Express venture at the start, as second-in-command to tough Denning Hartman. But Zennor had the problems of Hartman believing that they had crossed trails in the past, and the fact that he was strongly attached to Hartman's Indian girl, Conchita.

BLACK JO OF THE PECOS
Jeff Blaine
Nobody knew where Black Josephine Callard came from or whither she returned. Deputy U.S. Marshal Frank Haggard would have to exercise all his cunning and ability to stay alive before he could defeat her highly successful gang and solve the mystery.

RIDE FOR YOUR LIFE
Johnny Mack Bride
They rode west, hoping for a new start. Then they met another broken-down casualty of war, and he had a plan that might deliver them from despair. But the only men who would attempt it would be the truly brave — or the desperate. They were both.

THE NIGHTHAWK
Charles Burnham

While John Baxter sat looking at the ruin that arsonists had made of his log house, a stranger rode into the yard. Baxter and Walt Showalter partnered up and re-built the house. But when it was dynamited, they struck back — and all hell broke loose.

MAVERICK PREACHER
M. Duggan

Clay Purnell was hopeful that his posting to Capra would be peaceable enough. However, on his very first day in town he rode into trouble. Although loath to use his .45, Clay found he had little choice — and his likeness to a notorious bank robber didn't help either!

SIXGUN SHOWDOWN
Art Flynn

After years as a lawman elsewhere, Dan Herrick returned to his old Arizona stamping ground to find that nesters were being driven from their homesteads by ruthless ranchers. Before putting away his gun once and for all, Dan forced a bloody and decisive showdown.

RIDE LIKE THE DEVIL!
Sam Gort

Ben Trunch arrived back on the Big T only to find that land-grabbing was in progress. He confronted Luke Fletcher, saloon-keeper and town boss, with what was happening, and was immediately forced to ride for his life. But he got the chance to put it all right in the end.

JE